VALHALLA REIGN:
A VALKYRIE'S TALE

ELIZABETH REYNOLDS

Valhalla Reign:
A Valkyrie's Tale

By: Elizabeth Reynolds

To Ally. Until we meet again.

Foreword

Every religion has its beliefs on the world coming to an end. There are always signs that indicate that it is near. These endings cannot be prevented. As the worlds near the end of their time, things begin to change and become dark.

This is the same for the Norse beliefs. There will come a time when Asgard, the home of the gods, will come to end. This is when the Valkyries will have to stand up, pick up their weapons, and try to help hold back the inevitable.

There are several signs that will be seen as the end comes to passing. First there will be a murder of a beloved god. The murder will be by a trusted member of the court. This will occur early on.

There will be three long, cold winters with warmth in between. These winters will last for three years. During the winter, the worlds will be plagued with battle and death.

After winter passes, two wolves will take to the sky, eating the sun and moon. This will throw the worlds into darkness. This darkness will cause fear and confusion throughout the worlds.

A red rooster will warn the different worlds that Ragnarök is coming. Heimdall will sound the alarm by blowing his horn as loud as he can so that the Valkyries in Valhalla will hear the warning that the final war has started. The Valkyries and Einherjar (warriors that died honorably during battle) will pick up their swords to fight alongside the Aesir against the giants in hopes to drive them back.

All of the fallen Aesir will rise once more to fight alongside their brothers and sisters one last time. Odin, atop his horse, Sleipnir, will lead the army into battle on the battlefield of Vigrid.

As the gods and army are gathering, the giants, with Hel and all her dishonorable dead, will sail the ship, Naglfar, to the plains of Vigrid to join the final battle. Nidhug, the dragon, will fly above the battlefield to gather as many corpses as he can to help feed his never-ending hunger.

Jormungand, the Midgard serpent, will emerge from the ocean surrounding Midgard and splash poison in all directions. Surtr, the fire giant, will set Asgard and the Bi-Frost on fire. Fenrir Wolf will break free from his chains to spread death and destruction.

When the battle comes to an end, the gods and the giants will have perished in their mutual destruction of one another. A new world will rise from the sea, beautiful and green.

This is known as Ragnarök.

There is, however, one thing that wasn't taken into consideration. The Valkyries' ability to change the course of history.

CHAPTER 1

*E*verywhere I looked, there was smoke and *fire. Screams from the people of Asgard echoed off the walls of Valhalla. My heart raced as my sword connected with my opponents. I had to help hold them back to give Odin and the other gods time to get the people out. If we couldn't hold the enemies back, then all was doomed.*

Thunder rumbled and lightning flashed, I felt relief with the knowledge that Thor was amid the battle. The noise became almost unbearable. I wanted to cover my ears, but my training and will wouldn't allow it. Out of the corner of my eye, I saw my troops, one by one, hitting the ground. Dead. We were losing the fight rapidly. I prayed to the gods that they would be able to help save us from sudden death.

Then there was silence. It was as if everything had frozen in place. I looked around to see all my people had perished. We were losing. I knew that I had failed. I had one job, and I hadn't been able to do what needed to be done.

The icy hot pain of a sword entering my stomach was a shock to the system. I felt myself collapsing to lie with the rest of the fallen.

I jerked up, looking around my quarters. The others were still asleep, the room dark. I slipped out of bed and made my way out of the room. I didn't want to disturb my sisters and I knew that going back to sleep wasn't an option.

My heart pounded against my chest. The nightmare seemed real. It had felt like I had been stabbed. I rubbed my chest where the phantom pain lingered. It had been very vivid. That was not the first time I had a dream of that nature as of late. I was growing concerned.

I knew what I had to do. I needed to visit the Norns. They would be able to answer the questions that were starting to flood my mind. I needed to go before I had to start my duties. There was a battle in Midgard, and I was supposed to study the warriors.

Peeking out the window, I could see that the sun was just beginning to rise, so I would have time to visit the Well of Urd. I hadn't visited the fates for quite some time. I hoped they weren't too upset, but training and finding warriors worthy enough to help guard Asgard was time consuming.

I stepped out into the cool damp air. Taking a deep breath, I tried to forget the sense of foreboding that I had. Picking up the pace, I headed toward the well. I wanted to get out of Valhalla as quickly as possible. If I were seen, there would be questions. I had already been told I was being foolish. Being the youngest sister had several downfalls, especially when it came to being taken seriously.

The well was near the center of Asgard, not far from Yggdrasil. The Norns would likely be watering the roots of Yggdrasil, like they did every morning before they began their work, weaving the fate and destiny of the mortals below.

As predicted, the three women carried buckets of water toward Yggdrasil. One by one, they poured their bucket over the tree, then returned the buckets to the well. I glanced up in amazement at Yggdrasil. Every time I saw it, I felt awe wash over me. It was majestic in itself. The world tree. It could be seen in all nine worlds. It connected us all together. There was a magic in the tree that you could feel when standing near it. The magic felt like a pulse, warm against my skin. A rooster sat at the top of the tree. It would begin its call as the sun rose.

Waiting to be acknowledged, I stood as still as possible to cause as little disruption as I could. They took their chores seriously. There was rumor that Verdandi had a fit because she had been interrupted once and threw an Asgardian down the Well of Urd. He had never been seen or heard from again.

"Don't just stand there, Kara. You haven't got all day," Skuld said without looking in my direction. "Brynhild will be looking for you if you are gone too long."

Bowing to the Norns, I spoke softly. "Great ones, I come looking for solace and wisdom."

"You may get both here, what is troubling you, young one?" Urd asked.

"We know what is wrong with the child," Skuld scoffed. "It would hasten things if we just told her what she seeks."

"Why don't you two hush and let the child speak?" Verdandi said. She smiled at me. Her smile was toothless, yet harmless. It made me wonder how old she really was. I believed the stories that they had been around since the beginning of time. "What is it you need, child?"

"I've been having disturbing dreams. I need to know what it means." I shifted my weight from one foot to the other.

"Come closer, my dear, and tell us more." Verdandi signaled for me to sit at her feet.

I came closer and knelt in the soft grass at the roots of Yggdrasil.

"Yes, tell us these visions," Skuld whispered.

I began to tell them the dreams I had been having. When finished, I realized the Norns had grown silent. Glancing at them had my heart racing. They were just staring at me, looks of consternation upon their faces.

Skuld glanced over at Urd. "She has seen it then."

"Seen what?" I asked as Urd nodded.

Verdandi looked up toward the top of the tree and the rooster perched there. She didn't say a word, but a frown crossed her expression.

"What do I need to know?" I felt a tightness squeezing my chest. My heart beat against my ribs, forcing my breathing to pick up.

"It is going to come to pass." Skuld spoke so low, I had to strain to hear her.

"What is?"

"Ragnarök."

"Ragnarök?" I repeated stupidly. "That is just a story the elders tell young Asgardians to keep them in line and scare them at bedtime. It isn't a thing."

"If it isn't a thing, then why have you Valkyries been preparing your entire existence, yet have never picked up weapons in actual battle?" Urd's eyebrow rose with the question.

"It is just what we do." My mind whirled. Ragnarök couldn't be real. If it was, that would mean that the end was coming, and we were all going to die.

"You will see for yourself soon enough, young Valkyrie. Prepare for battle. When you retrieve warriors, only take the strongest warriors you can find. You will need it." Verdandi stared me in the eyes.

"Remember, you possess more power than you know. Now, you must get back. It is almost time for you to go to Midgard."

I stood, bowed, and walked back to Valhalla. I didn't believe in Ragnarök. It was just stories. There was no way that it was a real thing. Odin, Thor, and the other Aesir were too strong, too wise to let that happen. They could prevent something like the destruction of Asgard. Thor wouldn't let anything happen to Midgard either. Frigg would make sure we were all safe.

They would send us and the warriors out to ensure it. Ragnarök would not come to pass. I was going to have to brush up on the stories though, so I would know what to look for. Just in case. ***

"These mortals will never learn that they need to fight together, not apart. If they were to join forces, they would likely outnumber and outpower us." Mist glided through the field, carefully stepping over bodies of fallen who were not worthy of our offer.

"Mist, humans will never figure it out. They weren't made that way. If they did, they wouldn't need us. Then we would have fewer worthy warriors to bring home." I helped the soul of one warrior, to free him from his mortal body. He had fought valiantly until his last breath.

"Kara, if they would join forces, there would be more worthy souls to join us, not less. They wouldn't need to train as much once in Valhalla either."

I considered what Mist said. It made sense, but I still believed that they would no longer need us if they were to figure out how to work together as a species. Yet they never would figure it out. They were too busy fighting each other. If they stopped fighting each other, we wouldn't have any warriors to bring home.

We gathered up a few more souls and headed back home. Once we were standing at the Gates of Valhalla, we turned and looked at the souls. They stood there, looking around with mixed looks of awe and fear.

"Do not fear, mighty warriors. We have found you worthy and brought you to a warrior's paradise. Welcome to Valhalla, our home." I opened the gates and stepped aside to let them cross the threshold.

Once inside the walls, they would be whisked off by the Valkyries who were in charge of settling them into the barracks and explaining what was to be expected of them from here on out. It was a great privilege to be chosen for Valhalla and they would learn this.

Gunn approached me with a sly smile on her face. "Brynhild was looking for you this morn. You are to report to her at once."

I fought snarling at Gunn. She tended to like to see me get in trouble. She started to act in that manner after I bested her in hand-to-hand combat a fortnight ago. Since then, she did everything in her power to see me punished.

I made my way to the conference room where Brynhild was likely waiting. Opening the doors, I stepped inside.

"Close the doors." Brynhild commanded. She had her back to me, facing out the window.

I shut the door and stepped farther into the room, clasping my hands together behind my back. I felt anxious, not sure why she wanted to talk to me. I forced myself to stand still.

Slowly, she turned toward me, her black hair flashing purple in the sunlight. Her violet eyes shone. She stared at me as she came closer. Signaling for me to sit, she took a seat at the opposite side of the table.

Crossing to the table, I carefully sat on the chair, almost as if it were fragile. Waiting until she spoke was killing me. This was a control tactic, and she was likely seeing if I would break before she spoke. Brynhild was always putting me through tests like this.

"You were up and about early this morn."

"Yes, I'm sorry, I couldn't sleep so I thought I would go to Yggdrasil for a bit." I hoped my explanation would be enough for her.

"I've seen you toss and turn and cry out in your sleep. What is going on, Kara?"

Looking down at my hands, I studied my knuckles, which were still bruised from the last bout of hand-to-hand combat that I had been in. "I have been having bad dreams."

"Tell me about it."

As I explained the dreams I'd been having, I chanced a look up to see her watching me intently. She had a frown on her face while I described the dreams. They were so vivid that it was easy to describe them in great detail. I could still remember the smell of the burning houses and flesh. Visions of the nightmare flashed through my mind. As I wrapped up, I made sure to look her directly in the eye. "I am afraid that Ragnarök is on its way."

"Kara, you have nothing to worry about. *If,* and only if, Ragnarök is to come to pass, we will be warned and prepared. It is just a children's tale. It isn't going to happen."

I nodded. "Yes, Ma'am. Now, if you will excuse me, I have chores that need to be done."

"You are dismissed."

Standing, I turned and walked from the room before she had a chance to say anything else. I walked out to the practice field and became engaged in a bout of hand-to-hand combat with one of the newest warriors. He was a good fighter, but still green. When I had him on the ground, I pressed my boot into his throat. Looking down at him, I smiled.

"You did well, but you have much to learn if you plan on ever going to battle with Thor, God of Thunder, or become a guard of Asgard. Again."

Releasing his neck, I stepped back so he could stand. Instead, he made a spinning motion and swept my feet out from under me. I landed on the ground with a thump. The air was knocked out of me, and it took me a moment to catch my breath.

Arching my back, I shoved myself upward and flew back up to my feet. He threw a punch that connected with my jaw, then the fight began in earnest. I was letting out a little of my pent-up aggression. When I had him on the ground once more, he was unconscious. He fought very well that time. One thing the warriors had trouble learning was not to see me as a woman, but an opponent.

I planned on beating that habit out of him. In Valhalla and the battles, there would be no difference between men and women. The enemy was the enemy.

CHAPTER 2

The view into the outer reaches of Asgard was simply breathtaking. The clouds rolled gently in the sky, reflecting off the beautiful water. The Rainbow Bridge stretched across the water to the large structure that was the Bi-Frost. Beyond the Bi-Frost was the unknown. I always wondered what was out there and envied those who were able to come and go as they pleased.

I knew my duty was important, but I wished I had the freedom to roam as I pleased. I would have loved to be able to go on an adventure where I didn't have to collect souls and bring back the dead. I sighed and let my feet dangle over the ledge I was sitting on.

The sound of a pebble tumbling downward caught my attention. I leaned over the edge to see where it came from. I didn't think there was anyone above me, so the sound had to have come from below.

"Careful, would hate to see you fall." A deep voice rumbled from behind me.

I turned slowly to see large, heavy boots and armor-clad legs behind me. My eyes followed those legs up until they landed on a face. I stared into the golden face of Thor. My heart stuttered as uncertainty washed over me. I had never been that close to one of the Aesir before.

He smiled then reached a hand out to me. "Here, let me help you."

My hand trembled as I reached out to take his. I wasn't sure what to think about it. I had always heard that Thor had a temper on him and that he was rarely happy. His warm hand closed around mine as he helped me stand.

"Do you speak?" His brows furrowed while he stared at me.

"Aye, I speak, Majesty," I said softly.

"Are you well?"

Nodding, I spoke. "Yes, I just needed to clear my head. I'm sorry if I disturbed you."

"No, I apologize. I didn't mean to disturb you; you were clearly here first. I come up here to clear my thoughts as well." His eyes left mine. "It is beautiful, isn't it?"

"Yes, it is." I placed my right fist over my heart and bowed my head to show him the respect he deserved. "I shall leave you to your thoughts."

I stepped to the side, so I could go around him. Before I could walk past him though, he reached out and grabbed my arm. Reflex and training took over. I spun into him, my fist coming up to hit him square in the nose. He released my arm, taking a step back. I stared at him in horror with the realization that I had just hit not only the future king of Asgard, but the God of Thunder himself. I couldn't move from the shock of what I had done. I could be punished severely for that movement or worse, banished from Valhalla.

My heart was in my throat as I waited to see what his reaction was going to be. I prayed to Odin that he wouldn't be too angry with me. I hadn't thought before I reacted, instincts had taken over. Now I was going to be punished for it. I hoped that they wouldn't send me to Jotunheim or worse, Helheim. If I was deemed unworthy, I feared they could give me to Hel, then she would be able to do with me as she willed, which, knowing her, was torture. She liked to inflict pain on others.

He pulled his hands away from his face, blood covering his mustache, mouth, and into his beard. He then did something that I had least expected. He smiled at me.

"You have quite the arm on you," he said. "I'm going to guess that you are an infamous Valkyrie."

"I am so sorry, Majesty. Please forgive me. I forget myself."

He laughed. "No, it is I that apologize. I shouldn't have grabbed you. I have learned a lesson this day."

"You aren't going to have me banished?" I blurted out.

"Not this day. It is safe to say that I feel more comfortable meeting a Valkyrie that stands up for herself, even to me."

"Thank you." I rushed around him and started to descend the mountain.

"Wait," he called out.

I turned my head back to look at him.

"Can I have your name?"

"Kara."

"It was a pleasure meeting you, Kara."

I nodded again and hurried back down the mountain in hopes that we would both forget the unusual exchange. However, there was a tiny part of me that hoped I would run into him again.

***

Walking through the battlefield with Mist, I couldn't get my mind off a certain blond god. His eyes had haunted my dreams. I wanted to see him again, but

I hadn't told anyone about the interaction. It had been strange. Besides, I could get in trouble for what I'd done.

"Kara, where is your mind today? You seem to have your head in the clouds." She glanced at me sideways.

"Huh? Oh, nothing. I was just thinking."

"Thinking of a certain someone, are you?"

"No!" I said emphatically.

She laughed. "Do not fret so, Kara. I'm not going to tell anyone. Just remember that it is forbidden to take a lover. We are to remain pure of heart and body." She lowered her voice conspiratorially, "but it is okay to look."

"You are daft. There isn't anyone that I am looking at, romantically or otherwise. I am just... I don't know. I feel off. I need to get my head back in the game."

She stopped and stepped closer to me. Placing her arms on my shoulders, she pulled me into a hug. "Are the nightmares getting worse, sister?"

Shrugging, I stepped back. "I'm not sure. I can't shake it."

"It is just a dream. Dreams aren't real."

"It feels real, Mist." Shaking my head, I turned away. "Let's get this done. I'm wary."

We collected the souls in silence. As soon as we got back to Valhalla, I escaped back to my chamber. I crawled into my bunk and attempted to go to sleep. I was drained, physically and mentally.

***

The smoke burned my eyes and made me cough. I blinked several times, looking around. The bodies of my sisters were strewn about as if they were nothing except ragdolls. Blood seeped from their wounds. I stepped over them quickly, trying to find an escape.

There were screams off in the distance. The enemy had breached the city walls. They were in Asgard, killing the innocents. I ran in that direction, hoping to save some of them. If I could save even one person before I was killed, then my life wouldn't be given in vain.

As I entered the main city in Asgard, I could see the enemy storming houses. Villagers were fighting back and trying to protect their own, yet the women and children were unarmed and vulnerable. Racing into the heart of the battle, I fought with all that I possessed, yet I didn't feel like I was doing enough. I kept chanting in my head: save one life, save one life. I wanted to be able to say that I did that.

I watched as a sword arched toward a child. Jumping, I fell onto the blade, saving the little girl from an untimely death. I felt the cold metal enter my stomach, cutting through my insides. Blood seeped out of the corner of my mouth. My strength drained out of me, leaving me too weakened to stay on my feet. My legs gave out on me, dropping me to my knees. As the life slipped away from me, the image of a man flashed through my mind. Thor.

My body jerked as I sat straight up. Gasping, I tried to calm my erratic heart rate. I was shaking from the fear and adrenaline. I jumped out of bed. Pulling my boots on, I headed out of the bunker toward the mountains. I needed to clear my head and think about the dreams.

I knew what the Norns told me about them and Ragnarök, but the dreams kept ending in my death. I needed to know what that meant. Was I going to die when the enemy attacked? I climbed the trail to my spot. When I reached my ledge, I froze.

15

I wasn't alone. Thor was leaning against the rock wall, staring out into the vastness. I wasn't sure if I should keep going or if I should make my presence known. I began to back away when Thor spoke.

"You do not have to leave. Join me, please."

"Are you sure? I don't mean to intrude."

"It isn't an intrusion. I'm inviting you to join me. You sound like you need some solace. We do not have to speak, but some company would be nice." Pushing off the wall, he stepped toward the ledge, sitting. Then he looked at me and patted the ground beside him.

I sat down beside him, letting my legs dangle over the edge. Staring out at the water, my dream flashed through my mind again. I shook my head, trying to rid myself of the images. I didn't want to get worked up again. I couldn't afford to show any weakness, especially in front of the God of Thunder. It would be in bad form for him to see weakness.

I could feel warmth radiating from his arm beside mine. My skin soaked it up, hungrily. I hadn't realized how cold I felt until that moment. The adrenaline from the nightmare was starting to wear off. A shiver ran through me.

"What brings a Valkyrie out here at this time?" Thor asked, his voice soft.

Shrugging, I stared straight ahead. I wasn't sure what to tell him. "I just needed to think."

"Ah, that makes sense. I needed to think as well."

I turned my head to study him. He was staring out into the distance. His jaw was tight, like he was clenching his teeth. His shoulders were rigid, posture straight. There was tension radiating off him in waves. It was almost visible.

"Are you alright?" I couldn't help but ask him. I wasn't sure why I was worried about whether or not he was okay.

He sighed. "I am fine, thank you."

"You feel it too."

A golden eyebrow shot up, and his head slowly turned in my direction. "Feel what?"

"The unease."

"Aye, you could say that."

"Ragnarök is coming. I fear the worst."

"No, it isn't."

"I've been dreaming of it. I spoke with the Norns. They told me it is going to come to pass."

"The Norns? You've been to see them?"

I nodded.

"Tell me of your dreams."

With a deep breath, I began telling him the dreams, starting with the first one. Once I began speaking, I couldn't stop. I told him every detail that I could remember. I couldn't look at him while I was telling him about the dreams, so I stared out into the darkness while I spoke. Out of the corner of my eye, I could see the rainbow bridge. Random sparks were flashing on it in a mesmerizing pattern.

It surprised me how easy it was to talk to him. I always figured speaking to one of the gods would be difficult. I was under the impression that they didn't like to listen. I had been told they would never take the time to talk to a lowly Valkyrie like myself.

When I finished, I glanced in his direction. He was watching me still, shadows clouding his eyes. I didn't know what he was thinking, but if I looked close enough, it looked like there was lightning dancing in his pupils.

"I am going to look into this for you. I will find out what is going on. I wish that you didn't have the burden of those nightmares on your shoulders. I would take them away if I could."

"Thank you, Majesty."

"Call me Thor, Valkyrie."

"You may call me Kara then."

"Thank you, Kara. I am going to go to Odin at first light with what you have brought to my attention. We will get this squared away. I am going to make sure that this does not come to pass."

I gave him a nod, but I didn't think it would be as easy as he seemed to think. If the Norns were correct, our whole world was going to come crashing down, along with the deaths of everyone in Asgard. First the Aesir would perish, then the Asgardians.

CHAPTER 3

I tried to convince myself that I was just overreacting, but the knot in my stomach told me otherwise. Indecision weighed on my mind as I paced the bunker. I needed to find a way to ease my mind. The Norns had done nothing to help, they had just made me more uneasy.

I couldn't get the encounter with Thor out of my mind either. He made me uneasy for other reasons. Reasons I had never expected to feel. Desire. It was a foreign feeling for me. I had never felt anything but disdain for the male species, until now. I wasn't sure what to do with the feelings I had. I knew I would never be able to act on it; I supposed I would just have to ignore it.

I also had a hard time comprehending the fact Thor seemed to believe me. He didn't treat me as if I were simply a child or silly woman with a vivid imagination. If I had brought it to someone else, they may have just laughed my concerns off, like Brynhild did.

With my mind busy, I slipped out of the room. I needed to clear my head and refocus. It was important that I did so. When I entered the courtyard, it was hard to see. It was so dark, I could barely see my hand in front of my face. Blinking rapidly, I hoped my eyes would adjust to the blackness quickly.

Leaving Valhalla, I made my way toward the Bi-Frost and Rainbow Bridge. I wasn't sure why I headed in that direction, but I wasn't going to question my instincts. Thunder began to rumble before I made it to the Bi-Frost and shouts echoed through the streets. Heimdall's horn began to blare, sounding an alarm. Something major was happening.

Lightning lit the sky. I looked up to see the silhouette of a certain god flying through the air, hammer extended. I sped up, hoping to find out what was going on. I watched as he disappeared into the Bi-Frost.

My heartbeat thundered in my head in time with my feet hitting the ground. As I approached the Bi-Frost, I slowed and moved cautiously. I could hear voices of several men, Thor included. It sounded like there was confusion and anger in the room.

I slipped in without being noticed and kept to the shadows. I watched as the scene unfolded in front of me. A man was sprawled on the floor with the others surrounding him. It didn't take long to recognize him as Baldr.

Kneeling next to Baldr were Loki, the God of Mischief, and Heimdall. Heimdall had his horn lying beside him as he pressed his fingers to Baldr's throat. Thor towered over them, looking onto the scene.

"What is this?" he demanded. If I was correct, there was fear and definitely anger lacing his voice.

"Thor, I found him like this in Jotunheim. I brought him back immediately. I'm not sure what happened." Loki glanced up at Thor, then back down to the man on the floor. His hands had been pressed against Baldr's side, which was covered in blood.

Heimdall shook his head, slowly standing to rise. "He's gone. I'm sorry. I did not see this happen."

Thor clasped him on the back. His expression was solemn. "Thank you, my friend."

There was a heaviness that filled the air as Odin entered the Bi-Frost; Loki stood. I watched Odin cross to the men, his eyes appeared to be on his son, lying lifelessly on the floor. He stared at the body for several moments while the silence filled the room. He turned and faced the three men at the scene.

"Loki, my brother, what happened?" Odin's voice was scratchy from the bottled-up emotion.

"I am not sure, brother. I found him bleeding out in Jotunheim. I had heard rumor that an Aesir had been attacked, so I went to investigate. He was barely alive when I found him, so I brought him back as quickly as I could. I hoped that he could be saved once we got back." Loki glanced at the body, then back to the All-Father. "I will do everything in my power to find out who is responsible for this."

Odin gave him a curt nod. "When you find him, bring him to me. I will deal with him." He left in a whoosh of robes.

"Loki, go on up and clean yourself. I will have Baldr taken to be prepared for his last respects. We will then send him off on his final farewell." Thor took command of the room. Loki nodded at him and walked out. Once Loki was gone, Thor turned to Heimdall. "Tell me what you know, Heimdall. I know you are aware of more than what you let on. You see a great many things."

"I fear there is not much that I can tell you. Baldr did not head to Jotunheim originally. I'm not sure how he was found in Jotunheim. I haven't seen Loki in a while either. It makes me uneasy that he showed up the same time as Baldr's demise."

"Aye, but you know Loki as well as I. He wouldn't do anything to Baldr. He is practically our uncle. He has been around since we were babes."

Heimdall walked to the window, staring out at Asgard. Thor followed him until they were side by side, staring out into the lights of the city. "What I see is disconcerting."

I slipped deeper into the shadows so as not to be seen. I didn't want to eavesdrop, but it was too late for that. I should have made my presence known long before their private conversation. I tried to make myself as invisible as possible. I wished I hadn't made my way into the Bi-Frost, but I was here, and there was nothing more that could be done.

"You are not the only one. The Valkyries are on edge as well." Thor's voice was distant as if his mind wasn't in the room with them, but elsewhere.

Heimdall nodded. "Mayhap they need to be. Tis their job to prepare for Ragnarök. They have the sense needed to determine when it is the real thing."

"Aye. Help me keep an eye out. Keep me updated on any comings and goings." Thor turned toward Heimdall. "Do not speak of this conversation to anyone, Odin included. For the moment, it is best to keep this conversation between these walls and the two of us."

"That I can do, Thor. Rest assured that this conversation will not leave the room. Just remember there are always more than four ears in a room. Sometimes the walls have ears as well."

"Thank you, my friend. I must go break the news to Baldr's wife, Nanna. I fear that she may already know, and I expect the worst."

After Thor was gone, Heimdall turned in my direction, and looked straight into my eyes. "I know you are there, young Valkyrie. You can come out now."

I stepped from the shadows, nervous of what would happen, being that he knew I had been hiding and eavesdropping. If he told Thor or Odin, I could be put to death.

He smiled a soft smile at me, making me nervous. I expected sternness, not softness. "Relax, Kara. You forget, I see everything. You were meant to witness what you have."

"What do you mean?" I asked.

"All will be revealed soon enough." He led me to the window facing Asgard. "Look out there, child. This is your destiny. Thor is about to be consumed in great sadness. Things are forever changed. All we can do is prepare the best we can and be there for him."

"I'm just a Valkyrie, Heimdall. I am nothing to anyone. Just another sacrifice to the greater good."

He turned his head, looking down at me. "You don't believe that, or you wouldn't be here. You are special. I am not sure why or how, but you are. You are important to him. Just keep that in mind during the next few trials."

He turned from me, walking back to his post. I was clearly dismissed with much on my mind. As I walked from the Bi-Frost, thunder roared across the sky. It reminded me of a wounded lion that I had seen in Midgard. Lightning began to dance through the clouds. I walked faster, trying to get back to Valhalla before the rain began to fall. I didn't want to be caught in the downpour of Thor's grief.

I stopped at the fork in the road. I had the choice to walk into town to where I knew I would find Thor, or I could go home to Valhalla and pretend I knew nothing. Indecision flooded me. I stared at the two different paths, trying to decide the fate I would follow.

If I headed to Valhalla, I could pretend I knew nothing of what was going on and go back to the safety of my life. The road was tempting. I could easily head back and act like none of this had happened. If I did though, would I be able to live with myself?

If I took the path that led to Thor, what would my future hold? Things would never be the same. Heimdall's words echoed through my mind. *Things are forever changed.* Did that mean that I should take the path to Thor?

Rain began to fall in a light rain. I was torn. I knew where my head said I should go, but my heart and desire wanted to head to him. Be there as he fell apart. I shook my head. I needed to be rational, not emotional. I decided to head back to Valhalla. As I tried to take my first step, I couldn't get my feet to lift.

Thunder rumbled, and lightning flashed as the rain started to come down in a steady downpour. The water penetrated my clothing, thoroughly soaking me. Finally, I turned toward the town and headed to Breidablik, Baldr's house.

The house stood out like a beacon in the darkness. As lightning flashed, it reflected off the silver roof. Breidablik was the brightest house in all of Asgard. I stood at the base of the steps before I realized I had moved that quickly. Staring at the door, I slowly made my way up the stairs. My heart pounded louder with every step I took.

With a trembling hand, I reached up and pushed the door. It swung open without a sound. I stared into the dark house, hesitant to enter. I didn't know what I would do or say if I did go in. There would be questions that I didn't know how to answer. Even as I had convinced myself to turn away and head back to Valhalla, my feet led me inside. Traitorous bastards.

I followed the sounds of agony to the room that Nanna and Thor were in. He was sitting on the floor with her in his arms and she groaned in pain and clutched her chest. The cries coming from her mouth were the sounds of true heartbreak. I had never heard sounds so sorrowful.

I watched, frozen with sadness as the goddess gave up the will to live. As she died, she whispered Baldr's name. The life slipped from her while Thor held her tight. He looked up at me then. Tears glistening in his eyes.

My heart was shattered for the loss he was going through. I approached the pair and knelt beside him. No words were exchanged as I embraced him in a hug, trying to express how sorry I was and that I was there for him. I hoped he understood what I was trying to say.

He didn't move, didn't flinch as I wrapped my arms around his strong ones. I gently placed my head on his shoulder. He turned then, putting his nose in my hair and taking a deep breath. After what seemed like an eternity hugging him, he shifted.

Pulling back, I saw that he carefully placed Nanna on the floor and was wrapping his arms around my waist. Embracing me fully, I felt him bury his head in my neck. The warmth of the tears that escaped his eyes landed just above my collar bone.

I blinked rapidly, trying to fight back the tears that were threatening to spill from my eyes. I willed myself to stay strong for him. Suddenly, he lifted his head. With deep blue stormy eyes staring at me, Thor put his hand on the back of my head and brought his mouth to mine. His mouth tasted of salty tears and sadness.

He broke the kiss and looked me in the eyes. Then he whispered, "Thank you."

Chapter 4

The news of the death of one of the Aesir spread through Valhalla like wildfire. I had heard of the tragedy before I had even finished with the day's training. Everyone was in shock and mourned the death of Baldr. He was a well-respected and gentle god. The weight of his death still weighed heavily on my soul.

Whispers began, stating the fact that Baldr hadn't been brought to Valhalla. As an Aesir and great warrior, his spirit should have been brought to us. We had welcomed some of the other Aesir that had died during battles or other ways. Never had we not had one come to us.

Nanna's death wasn't as talked about as Baldr's. It was almost as if she were just an afterthought. It wasn't that she wasn't important, she was. Nanna was an extension of Baldr. Their love had been a love to look up to. They were two entities that had become one. It made sense that she had passed when he did.

I felt the unease while we sat at the table eating dinner. I bit into my boar leg as I listened to the conversation around the table. There was talk of Baldr, but it was what else I heard that caught my full interest.

I chewed and pretended not to be paying attention, but I couldn't bring myself to stop listening.

"I heard Thor has been to the Norns today. He is also investigating the death of his brother. He has gone to Odin about something that put Odin on edge so badly that he locked himself in his study the rest of the day after they found Baldr. Some say that he is mourning, others are saying that he is preparing to attack the giants. But the servants are saying that it is more than that." Hlokk told Gunn.

"That's interesting. I wonder what it is that Thor told him to make him act in such a manner. Maybe Thor is going back to Midgard. I heard that he had found a mortal there that he has fallen in love with and is planning to bring back here." Gunn responded.

Thor had gone to the Norns? He was taking me seriously. I hadn't truly expected him to look into it. My heart fluttered and stomach flipped. No one had paid that much attention to me before. I was the youngest of the Valkyries, so my sisters tended to treat me as if I wasn't there or didn't know what I was doing.

"I have also heard that someone caught his interest, but I don't believe it was a mere mortal. I hear that it is someone more powerful than that. Thor is keeping his business close to his chest though, no one seems to know exactly what he is doing. He is so mysterious."

I tuned out their chatter after that. I didn't want to hear how they thought he was handsome and would love it if he would bed them. Most of us had our virtue intact, but not all of us. The Valkyries who weren't pure had jobs of keeping the men entertained while the rest of us prepared and collected more warriors.

I had vowed that I would keep my virtue because I never wanted to become a toy for the warriors that lived here. You didn't get a choice if they wanted to rut into you. Once you gave yourself, you were basically up for grabs. The women who had taken that path didn't mind the multiple partners. I, however, found the thought of multiple partners repulsive. If I were honest, the thought of anyone touching me, besides one particular person, was appalling.

After dinner, the others retired to the bunkers or other places inside the stronghold, I headed out to the stables. I was hoping to clear my mind and get some sleep without nightmares. When I approached my horse's stall, I opened the door and stepped in. I pulled it shut behind me, then approached the beautiful white mare in front of me. She snorted at me as I approached.

Rolling my eyes, I offered her the carrot that I held in my hand. She ate it in two bites as I stroked her muzzle. Her hair felt like silk under my hand. She had been a gift from my parents before I was left at the stronghold. Her blue eyes shone at me.

I grabbed the brush, without saying a word, and began to brush her coat. I worked my way down her side to her wing. I tapped her twice, and she stretched it out so that I could brush under it. When I finished that side, I went to the other, repeating the process there as well.

"Good girl, Astrid. That's a girl," I stroked the horse carefully.

Setting the brush down, I cupped her face, resting my forehead on her. Being with Astrid tended to soothe my soul. I felt myself centering and calming down just by being near her.

A creak caught my attention. My eyes popped open and I was on alert. I knew I was no longer alone in the stable. I wasn't sure who or what was behind me, but I was ready for any situation. I felt a hand hovering above my shoulder. Spinning, I swung my arm out, knocking the hand nearing me away. I swung the other arm, fist connecting with my assailant's jaw.

My fist was reared back, ready to strike again, when I realized who I had attacked. Thor. Heat rushed to my face. I couldn't believe that I attacked him yet again.

Thor caressed his jaw as he spoke, "We must stop meeting like this, Valkyrie."

"I apologize. What are you doing here, Majesty?" My eyes darted around the stables.

"I came to speak to you."

My eyebrows rose. "You came to Valhalla just to speak with me?"

He gave me a slight nod. "I wanted to tell you what I have discovered."

"Is it true that Baldr is gone?" My stomach knotted as I waited for his answer.

He swallowed like the thought pained him before he spoke. "Yes. I am looking into that as well."

I crossed my arms over my stomach. If one of the Aesir was gone, I feared the worst.

Thor stepped closer to me, forcing me to raise my face to look up into his eyes. "I will get to the bottom of this. I have spoken with the Norns, and plan on speaking to them once more. I want you to be well prepared for anything. Do you think you can get the other Valkyries to make sure everything is in order for the war that is likely to come?"

I nodded. "I saw the red rooster this morn. It was in the place of the rooster that wakens Asgard."

"Yes, I saw it as well." He cupped my face with one hand. When he spoke again, his voice dropped an octave and gentled. "We just need to make sure that we have the upper hand. Be prepared for anything. If this is Ragnarök, you know what will happen."

"Aye, I do. We will all perish."

His hand on my face kept me from looking down. He leaned down, so his lips were a breath from mine. "I have no intention of dying, or letting you perish either. We are stronger than a prophecy."

I swallowed, my tongue darting out to wet my lips, which had become suddenly dry. My stomach was flipping with him so close. "Thor, there is no way to beat a prophecy. We just have to pray that it doesn't take us all out."

"That is where you are incorrect. A prophecy, is just an event that hasn't occurred yet. It is not set in stone. I believe that we are able to make our own futures, no matter what the prophecy says. We must change a few things to keep it from coming to pass as predicted."

"Like what?" My lips trembled. I brought my lower lip into my mouth and bit down on it to stop the quivering.

"Joining forces. Working together. See, you have already changed the future by bringing your concerns to me. The prophecy didn't mention anything about a fiery Valkyrie that would enter the mind of a certain god. There wasn't supposed to be any warning beside the physical signs of Ragnarök. You have taken the first steps to change our future." He brought his mouth down to mine.

The kiss caught me off guard. I attempted to step away, but his hand on my face kept me in place. After a moment, my stomach began to calm, just as another sensation began to overtake me. A warmth was spreading through my body, making me yearn for more. I melted into the kiss. His free hand slid around my waist, pulling me into him. My arms automatically wrapped around his neck.

When he broke the kiss, I was out of breath. My heart raced; knees were weak. He put his face down into my neck and shoulder. His breath sent tingles racing across my body. I wasn't the only one that was trying to catch my breath.

Thor straightened and smiled at me. "I feel as if I should apologize, but I do not intend to."

"One should not apologize for having a passion," I whispered. "However, that should not happen again. I mustn't. I mean, I can't do that again. I have to live a life of purity."

"Not all Valkyries are pure."

I raised an eyebrow at him. "That is true, however those who aren't pure, are made to become the warriors' whores. I do not wish to be one that has to pleasure the warriors here. I find rutting with multiple partners revolting."

"The Valkyrie Kara, if we were to do more than a simple kiss, it wouldn't be rutting." He brought my hand to his lips, placing a light kiss on the top of it. "And you wouldn't have multiple partners. However, I feel this is a discussion for another time. I must be going."

I watched as he left the stables, the breath I had been holding whooshing out of me. I turned to look at Astrid to see her just staring at me.

"What? Do you expect me to let him bed me within a moment's notice and become a whore to the gods?"

The horse snorted, then turned her head to the side. Walking out of the stall, I shut it behind me. When I turned back, there was a man standing there, staring at me with an unnerving smile on his face. He had long dark hair, and skin the color of fresh milk. His eyes were dark, almost soulless.

"So, this is what my nephew has been up in knots over. You don't look that impressive, Valkyrie, but to get into the mind of the Mighty Thor is some feat. It takes more than a pretty face to get his attention these days. He used to amuse himself with the whores at the palace. Now he ignores them all. I am not sure what you did that got his fancy."

"What are you doing here?" I asked.

Loki had put me on edge with the tone that he used. What he was saying was disgusting as well. I didn't want to believe that Thor used the whores of the palace, but a small voice in my head told me that I was being stupid. Of course, he did. He was a man, a god. He had needs. He was the ultimate warrior in my eyes.

"I wanted to see the amazing Valkyrie that has Thor up in knots, believing the end is near. Risking his father's wrath by coming into Valhalla. You know that this place is off limits to the Aesir."

"Then why are you here?" I crossed my arms, but stayed ready for anything. "If Valhalla is off limits, then I shall walk you to the gates. You need to leave."

"Ah, there is the fire that Thor would find intriguing. I am only here to make sure that my dear nephew isn't getting in too deep." Loki stepped closer to me. "You must be the warriors' Valkyrie, because you are too pretty and petite to be a fighter. Let me see what the interest is about."

He backed me against the wall, bringing his face down toward me. My hand came up, palm out. It connected with Loki's nose in a satisfying crunch. He backed off, cursing and covering his face.

"You bitch! I will teach you some manners yet."

"Do not touch me again. I will not tolerate being disrespected. I am a Valkyrie of Valhalla, one of the chosen by Great Odin himself to train the warriors of

33

Valhalla. I deem whether the warriors are worthy to be invited to Valhalla. Not to be touched by anyone."

He stepped closer to me, then struck me across the face with an open hand. Being caught off guard, I stumbled to the ground. Astrid began to stomp and huff. She reared, hitting the door of the stall hard enough that it broke. She charged Loki. Right before she headbutted him, he vanished.

I carefully got to my feet. Astrid nudged me with her nose. I put my hand on her face, stroking her gently to calm her. Once she was calm, I led her back to the stall. After replacing the door, I made my way to the bunkers and my cot. I hoped sleep would come quickly.

As I approached my room, Mist stopped me by grabbing my arm and turning me back to her. I didn't speak, just stared at her.

"Come with me." she said quietly.

I followed her back down the hallway. We turned and entered a small closet where we could talk in relative privacy.

"What happened?" She put her fingers under my chin and examined my face.

I shrugged. Struggling with indecision, I wasn't sure what to say. The truth didn't seem like the best idea, but she was my best friend and I wanted to tell someone. I studied Mist. She had been in my life for as long as I could remember.

Her hair was the color of the blue sky. I still wasn't sure how her hair was that hue. She claimed she was born with it, but it seemed odd to me. She was several inches taller than me. Her eyes were the same shade as her hair.

"You know you can tell me. It won't leave this room."

"I had an altercation with Loki."

"Loki?" Her eyes widened. "Did you leave the stronghold again to run into him?"

Shaking my head no, I glanced down. "I was in the stables with Astrid when he approached me. He got too close, so I struck him. He struck back. End of story."

"Kara, don't lie to me. There is more to the story than that. I can see it in your eyes. I have known you all your life. I know when you aren't being truthful. Why would Loki show up in the stables?"

"He followed Thor."

Her eyes widened. "Thor? As in the God of Thunder?"

"The one and the same."

"Why was he here?"

That part was tricky. I didn't know what to say. Telling her that Thor came to see me could be disastrous. The implications of him coming to see me could make our motives questionable. No one else knew about the dreams I had either, so I couldn't tell her that. Mist knew that I hadn't been sleeping well but wasn't fully aware of the situation.

I had taken too long to answer. Mist grabbed my hands, squeezing. When she spoke, her voice was barely above a whisper. "You know you can tell me anything. It won't leave this room. You can trust me."

I nodded. She was right, I could trust her. "He came to tell me that the rumors were true. Baldr is dead. His spirit hasn't come back to us. Thor fears that something is coming, and we need to be ready."

"Is that all that happened? Surely, Loki wouldn't have stuck around if he was just passing a message on to you. And why you? No offense, but you are like the lowest ranking Valkyrie here. Why wouldn't he go to Brynhild?"

I sighed. "I do not know. Maybe he came to the first Valkyrie that he could find?"

Mist glared at me. "Lies. The truth."

"I've approached him about the feelings I've had. He looked into it. He wanted to tell me what he had found."

"Now we're getting somewhere." She smirked. "What else? You are turning red, Kara."

"He kissed me." I admitted. I felt the heat rising in my face. "But that is all that happened. I put a stop to it. He will not touch me again."

Her eyes were wide, mouth open in an *O* shape. "How was it? I can only imagine what Thor kisses like."

"It was–pleasant."

"I'm sure it was more than pleasant, but we will need to talk about this later. Next time we go to Midgard, you and I are talking."

I nodded. It felt good to talk to someone about it. Maybe I would tell her everything.

CHAPTER 5

I awoke in a cold sweat. Sitting up, I felt disoriented, unsure of what was wrong. Glancing around the room, I saw the other Valkyries were also beginning to rise for the day, silence looming over us. I climbed off of my cot and slid my boots on.

As I was walking across the room, I realized what was wrong. It was still dark out. The dawn should have been breaking the darkness, bringing light to the sky. I made my way outside to find that not only were the Valkyries confused, but the warriors also stood out in the training yard, staring at the sky.

I felt the warmth of someone stepping up beside me. Out of the corner of my eye, I saw Mist standing there, hugging herself. She didn't appear to be the tough warrior that she was, she looked like a scared woman. I felt the fear in the pit of my stomach, but I couldn't let myself embrace it.

The sky was dark, no stars, no moon. I couldn't even see any clouds. It appeared that all the light had been stolen from Valhalla. I wanted to see if it was just Valhalla that was blanketed in darkness or if all of Asgard was affected.

"I need everyone to remain calm. I am sure this is nothing," Brynhild announced. "We will continue our day as normal. Odin will surely be able to fix whatever caused this darkness."

"How can Odin fix there being no sun?" I asked without thinking.

All eyes turned to me. Brynhild glared at me for several heartbeats before speaking again. "Odin is our god, our savior. He can make anything happen. It is in your best interest not to question Odin again."

I gave a slight nod. I wasn't going to push her any more than I already had. I also knew that I couldn't make an argument that didn't sound like I was questioning Odin or that I didn't worship Odin like I should.

Brynhild turned her eyes from me. "As I was saying, we will go about our normal routines even though it is dark. It will be beneficial for our warriors to be able to battle in the dark as well as the light."

Once dismissed, I made my way to the entrance of Valhalla. I was going to find out if this was one of the signs or if there was something we weren't aware of going on. I slipped through the door that led into Asgard.

Entering the city, I kept to the back roads that led to Yggdrasil. I wasn't sure why I felt that I needed to keep to the shadows considering it was dark, but I did. I wanted to make it to Yggdrasil unnoticed. The city was eerily silent. My footsteps echoed as I walked down the dirt trail. The fear coming from the houses was palpable. I almost felt like the fear was trying to strangle me.

I approached Yggdrasil to find the Norns perched in their usual positions, weaving the threads of life of the mortals. They didn't appear to have a care in the world. They worked methodically and carefully so as to not miss a beat in the weaving process.

Skuld looked up and stared at me, hands never stopping. She raised an eyebrow as I stood there, waiting.

"Speak, child," she rasped out.

"It really is happening, isn't it?" I asked. I felt like a scared little girl just finding out that the monsters were actually real and ready to eat me.

"We told you it would come to pass, yet you didn't believe us. Now it is quickly approaching." Urd said from her spot at the base of the tree. She didn't look in my direction, but it felt like she was staring at me.

"The mortals in Midgard are starting to be affected by the darkness," Verdandi added.

A chill ran down my spine. I couldn't imagine how the mortals were being affected, but it couldn't be good. "Is there something we can do? How bad is it affecting the mortals?"

"There is no stopping Ragnarök. Only hope for the best but be prepared for the worst. The mortals will do as they will. That is their way. They react without thinking, then suffer the consequences later. Pray that the darkness doesn't enter all the mortals or Midgard will be lost." Skuld explained. Her hands stopped as her eyes bore into mine. "You need to go. Don't forget that you need to dress for the winter. It is fast approaching. The cold will seep into your bones until you believe you are going to freeze from the inside out."

With that, the Norns turned their attention back to their weaving, leaving me with more questions than answers. I headed back toward Valhalla when a thought hit me. I had to know just how bad the mortals were being consumed by the darkness.

I turned to the left instead of right at the fork in the path, heading to the Rainbow Bridge and Bi-Frost. I was going to find out how bad it was, hopefully without the others finding out that I went down without permission.

I entered the Bi-Frost to find Heimdall standing there, staff in hand. Without a word, he led his way to the platform, slowly inserting the staff into a hole in the floor and twisting it until it clicked. The room began to turn slowly. Suddenly there was an opening in the side of the room that hadn't been there moments before, the Rainbow Bridge leading the way.

"Just call when you wish to return. I will be watching, young Valkyrie. I hope you find the answers that you seek." Heimdall nodded to me.

I gave him a nod back and walked to the doorway. I closed my eyes and shifted into a swan before flying through the opening to ride the Rainbow Bridge down to Midgard. I agreed with Heimdall. I hoped that the answers I needed would be revealed.

***

The first thing I noticed when I made it to Midgard was the sky. It was overcast and dark as well. I was shocked to see the darkness had physically spread there as well. I took to the sky, watching the land below. I was shocked by the scene before me.

Battles. They were everywhere. It looked like Midgard was in the process of destroying itself. The mortals were fighting amongst themselves, more than normal. Landing in a tree, I perched on a branch so I could watch the scene before me without detection.

The battle I was observing wasn't a fair one. It was one woman with long black hair, against three men with large weapons. She was holding her own well. She had a look of determination on her face as she fought with an intensity that I have seen in only a few of the warriors that were brought to Valhalla.

Another man started to approach from behind. I wanted to call out to the young warrior, but that was forbidden. I was only to observe. I wasn't allowed to interfere. Sending my thoughts in her direction, I hoped that she would sense the fourth before it was too late.

The woman turned just as the new man lunged toward her, but he didn't have a chance to stop her. A black blur hit the man in the side. They hit the ground, rolling. The woman took out another opponent in one swift swing. She had a small blade in her hand.

My eyes moved back to the blur and other man. It was a large feline. I believe it was called a jaguar. I wasn't entirely certain about the species that lived on Midgard. The animal's teeth pierced the skin of the man's throat, ripping it out in one bite. Blood spurted everywhere, soaking the animal with the man's blood.

With the aid of the large cat, the woman took out the rest of her opponents. Before my eyes, the animal disappeared, bones and body transforming into a man. The man had dark brown hair, with dark eyes. He still had blood all over the upper half of his body. He was a shifter. I hadn't realized that Midgard had those there as well. I had always believed that Valkyries and Tricksters were the only ones able to change form.

He looked down at the woman. "Are you okay, Sarah? I tried to get here faster."

"I'm good, Parker. Really. I think I could have handled them on my own." The woman smiled at him.

"Get real. I saved your ass. You would have been demon food if I hadn't showed up."

"You're a good big brother. Feel better now?"

"Yeah." The man smiled, but it faded quickly. "What do you think is going on? Mom said there was an influx of demonic activity, and the humans are crazier than usual. What triggered them? I'm sure she knows, but she is being tight-lipped."

The woman shrugged. "No idea, but I agree, it is weird. She has been saying for years that the war was going to get worse before it gets better though. Maybe that's what she meant. I just hope that it gets better before everyone ends up dead."

"Same."

"Now, let's get going. I can't help but feel like we are being watched."

With that, they took off. I stayed motionless, trying to absorb everything I had learned. There were more than the mortals, humans as the woman named Sarah called them, on Midgard. They were feeling the effects of Ragnarök as well. What I had trouble comprehending was why they were fighting demons. They belonged in Helheim. Why were they on Midgard?

I took flight once more. My time away from Valhalla was limited and I hadn't learned much. I watched several unarmed men, women, and children being killed for no apparent reason. After seeing several deaths, I went back to where the Rainbow Bridge met Midgard. Silently, I called for Heimdall. It was the best way to get back without anyone realizing I had left Valhalla and Asgard altogether.

When I returned, my heart was heavy. I walked into the Bi-Frost, staring down at my feet. Boots stood before me; I raised my head to meet the dark, knowing eyes of Heimdall. He nodded once. I returned his nod with one of my own.

"It is true. Midgard is becoming dark as well. All the worlds will be dark in no time." I whispered.

"That is what I fear. Being prepared will help us all in the end. Knowing what to expect will also help us. I believe that and know you do as well. We will do what we can to save Asgard, the people, and Midgard."

"Did you know they have others besides mortals on Midgard?" My eyes stayed steady on his.

"I have seen some unusual things on Midgard, so I'm not terribly surprised."

"Did you know about the demons invading Midgard?"

He hesitated. "I am not surprised by that either."

"Why aren't they in Helheim?"

"Someone has released them."

I knew he wouldn't give me the answer I was seeking, so I simply nodded and walked around him to leave. He stopped me at the entrance of the Bi-Frost.

"Valkyrie, there is plenty you have yet to learn, but taking the initiative to learn even with the circumstances takes great strength."

Not sure how to respond, I simply left. I was making my way back to Valhalla when I heard voices that caught my attention. I was sure it was Loki, but I didn't recognize the other voice. I went a little closer in order to hear the conversation better.

"It has already begun," Loki said.

"You better not be wrong about this, Loki," the other voice warned.

"I am not wrong. I took care of Baldr myself. We shall continue as planned."

"What about Thor? He has been getting close to discovering the truth."

"That dumb oaf? He believes everything I say. He won't be a concern for long. Have you contacted her yet? Is she ready?"

"She will be ready when the time is right, you know this. She will not be rushed. The timing must be perfect."

"Now, you must go. I cannot be caught with the likes of you."

I backtracked as quickly as possible, so I could remain unnoticed. Arms went around my back and chest. I struggled to break free, hoping Loki wouldn't notice the exchange, but the voice behind me chilled me to the bone.

"Look what we have here. Thor's little girlfriend." Loki whispered in my ear.

I shouldn't have been surprised that he was able to sneak up on me. He was the Trickster God. I knew better than to let my guard down.

"Release me at once," I demanded.

"Why would I do that? It will be so much easier to take care of you now, since I'm sure no one knows where you are."

Stomping on his foot, I managed to break his hold. It was time for my training to be put to good use. This was going to be a fight for my life.

CHAPTER 6

Balling my hands into fists, I prepared myself for a battle that would likely end in my death. I was determined not to go down without a fight though. He was going to have to work to end my existence.

Loki laughed as he pulled a sword out of his robes. I wasn't sure where he had kept it, but figured it was some of his magic that kept it concealed. The fight was going to be unfair, but I knew I was a good fighter. Watching him, I slowly began to circle, trying to get into a position where my back was semi-guarded.

Loki swung his sword at me. I dropped to the ground to avoid being hit by the sharp metal. Sweeping my legs out, I kicked his feet from under him. He landed on his back with a thud. We both jumped to our feet.

I threw a punch he didn't expect, my fist connecting with his nose. There was a satisfying crunch and the warmth of blood gushed from his nostrils onto my hand. His arm came up, hitting me on the side of the head with the broad side of his sword.

Dazed, I stumbled backwards but managed to keep my feet. As the ringing in my ears faded, Loki disappeared. I spun, looking all around for him. When I didn't see him, I stopped moving and studied the area. I couldn't figure out where he had gone.

A weight suddenly dropped onto my back, knocking me to the ground. His hands came around my throat. He began to squeeze as I struggled to get away from him. My hands grabbed his, trying to get him to loosen the grip on my neck.

When that didn't work, I reached a hand up, raking my nails down his face as hard as I could. He yelled, his grip loosening enough for me to break his hold on my neck. I bucked and twisted my hips like a bull to get him off me.

There was a crash of thunder that caused us both to freeze. Lightning danced across the sky as clouds rolled in, covering the already black sky. Standing above us was Thor, floating in the air. Lightning flashed, and thunder roared with his wrath.

Reaching down, he grabbed Loki by the back of the neck, lifting him off me with one hand.

"What is the meaning of this?" Thor demanded, voice rough with anger.

"Thank Odin you are here, Thor. This Valkyrie has lost her mind. She attacked me without provocation. I feared for my life, so I fought back. I was just going to restrain her until I could get her back to Valhalla for the other Valkyries to do with her as they deem necessary. It is a death sentence to attack someone of the court," Loki stared at Thor like he was willing him to believe the lies.

Thor's eyes never left Loki as he spoke. "What is the truth, Kara?"

I bit my lip, then told Thor what I overheard, including how Loki took care of Baldr. When I finished recounting the events, I glanced at Thor's eyes to see they had hardened as he glared at Loki. His blue eyes were the color of dark clouds. I wasn't sure if the thunder I heard rolling in the distance was actually far away, or coming from inside of the god in front of me.

"Not only did you kill an Aesir, you lied to me; you betray the throne of Odin. Loki, that is treason and punishable by death. We will lock you away until Odin is able to come up with an appropriate punishment." Thor leaned closer, "By Odin's beard, I will see you suffer for the death of my brother, *Uncle*." He turned and began to give orders to the guards that were with him. I hadn't noticed them until just then. "Take him to the dungeons. Do not let him get away. You know his tricks. If he escapes, it will be your heads."

Once they left, Thor turned to me, stepping so close I could smell the scent that was uniquely him. He smelled of rain and new beginnings. His free hand came up and rested on my shoulder. "Are you well, Valkyrie Kara?"

"Aye, thank you, Thor, Son of Odin. I appreciate the assistance, even though I could have handled it myself." I smiled at him.

He returned my smile with one of his own. "I'm sure you could, little Valkyrie, but it was not necessary with me around."

His mouth came down and he gently placed a kiss on my forehead. His beard tickled my face. The simple gesture sent a sensation through me that I had never felt before. My stomach flipped, the hair on the back of my neck tingled, and goosebumps raced down my back, arms, and legs.

"I will need you to come with me to the Golden Palace, so you can tell Odin what you witnessed."

My eyes widened. Going to the palace meant that it would be out that I had left Valhalla and they would know I went to Midgard. My heart began to pound in

47

my chest. I felt like it was going to explode out of me. Sweat beaded up at the base of my spine. "Pardon?"

"You needn't fear. You will be fine. We will just tell Odin what transpired here, what you heard, then you will be free to return to Valhalla." His hand slid down to mine, giving me a reassuring squeeze.

I nodded once, swallowing around the lump in my throat. I knew I had to do my duty to Odin and the Aesir, but I was afraid of what they would say when they found out that I hadn't been doing my duty.

Thor turned and headed back toward the palace, my hand in his. I followed behind, wishing I could just disappear into the darkness and not have to go through this. Memories pushed to the surface of my mind as we walked. My parents, the few years I had with them before I was sent to train. Those memories were scarce but comforting.

Stay strong. Remember, Kara, you are destined for greatness. You will do amazing things. Trust your instincts and they will never lead you astray. Your destiny will be shown to you when the time is right. The words my mother told me, as she left me at the training compound and headed off to battle with a few of the others that never returned, stayed with me.

As we approached the Golden Palace, I was awestruck at how amazing it was up close. The gold seemed to shimmer, even in the darkness. We walked up the steps, Thor's hand tightening on mine, probably to make sure I wouldn't try to make a break for it. My free hand came up and rested on his bicep right above the crook of his elbow.

When we entered the palace, he set Mjolnir down on a table. We walked through the halls, toward the throne room. Light reflected and bounced off the golden walls and ceiling. Our bootsteps echoed through the halls. Out of the corner of my eyes, I saw staff and others staring at us.

Thor pushed the doors to the throne room open. As we stepped over the threshold, all conversation and music stopped. Every eye turned to us. Odin sat on his throne, dressed in a golden robe that matched everything in the room. He sat up a little straighter as we approached. The only thing that wasn't gold on him was his hair, which was stark white.

We stopped when we approached the end of the dais. I had never been this close to the All-Father, the Almighty Odin. I studied him, noticing that he had scars on his face and hands. He had been through several battles in his time, always coming out superior. He had a scar down the right side of his face that went across his eye. I wasn't sure how he could see out of that eye, or if he even could.

"Thor, what gives us the honor of your presence?" Odin asked. He stared straight at me, then down to our joined hands. "And with a Valkyrie, no less."

"Father, we came with news about Baldr's death and the one responsible." Thor explained without looking away. "I have brought the Valkyrie to see you because she witnessed an account of what happened with Baldr."

"What is it?" Odin's full attention was now on me.

I stepped to the side, letting go of Thor's hand. If I were going to recount what happened and face Odin, I was going to do it on my own, not cowering behind a man. "Majesty, I apologize for having to bring this news to you. And I am truly sorry for the loss of Baldr. His demise has been felt throughout not only Asgard, but Valhalla as well."

He nodded once. "He is training with the Valkyries then?"

"I'm sorry, we haven't seen him. We have round the clock watches, keeping an eye out for him. We also have Valkyries that are out searching for his soul." The flash of sadness in his eyes made my heart ache for him. "I did overhear the one who claims responsibility for Baldr's death, however."

Leaning forward, Odin's gaze intensified. "Do tell me. Everything."

"I overheard the god, Loki, speaking with someone I cannot identify. He was telling this being that he took care of Baldr and that they needed to proceed with the plan. He then asked if she was ready." I explained.

His brows drew together into a frown. "She who?"

"Forgive me, Majesty, I am not sure who she is. They never mentioned a name aloud."

"Go on."

I explained what happened after that, then Odin went on to ask me several more questions about different aspects of the conversation I had overheard and what I had seen. I answered his questions to the best of my ability, but I wasn't able to give him the information that he was truly seeking.

He sat back in his chair and stroked his white beard. "One further question, Valkyrie."

"Majesty?" My stomach dropped. This was what I had been afraid of.

"How did you happen upon this incident? You were supposed to be in Valhalla, training."

"Father, I do not see –" Thor started, but Odin silenced him with a glare.

I kept my back straight and my head up as I spoke. "When we awoke this morn, I noticed that it was dark. Some of the Valkyries and warriors were confused as to what was going on. I took it upon myself to attempt to seek answers as to where the light had gone. I visited the Norns."

"What did you find out, Valkyrie?"

The way he said Valkyrie made me feel like it was an insult instead of the honor that being a Valkyrie truly was. I was part of the elite group. There were only a few of us, so I was confused by the tone.

"I have been forewarned that the Coming is approaching, that we need to heed the warnings and prepare for the final battles of Asgard." My eyes were staring directly into his.

He threw me off guard because he laughed. It was a deep belly laugh. I felt the frown form on my face as I stared at him.

"This is too precious. The Valkyrie that Thor has taken a shining to is the same Valkyrie that knows what happened to my son. Child, you are putting too much power into children's stories. Ragnarök is not coming to pass." He eyed me up and down. "She doesn't look like much either, a slip of a woman."

Anger burned through me, making my face feel hot. My hands balled up into fists. I had to keep my cool though, this was the All-Father, the lord of the Valkyries. It would not be wise to let that anger loose on him.

"Father, she is more than what she appears. You mustn't judge her on her size, Kara has quite a bit of power behind her. Now, we must turn our focus to the important matter of Loki and his betrayal." Thor interceded.

"Yes," Odin sighed. "This is quite the quandary. Loki and I have taken a blood oath of brotherhood."

"Father, he betrayed that oath when he *murdered* your son." Thor's face began to redden.

"Aye, I am well aware of the situation, Thor. For the time being, Loki shall remain imprisoned until I am able to conceive a suitable punishment for his treachery."

Thor nodded curtly and led me from the room. We didn't speak again until we were out of the Golden Palace. We continued to walk until we were at the midpoint between the Golden Palace and Valhalla. He stopped and turned to me.

"I apologize for my father's behavior. He can be quite arrogant and flippant when it suits him."

I shook my head. "It's fine, Thor. I have heard worse. You forget that I train with the other Valkyries and warriors. I know my worth."

"Good." A smile formed at the corner of his mouth. "Now, I shall be a true gentleman and walk you to the gates of Valhalla."

"That isn't necessary," I took a step away from him. I didn't want him to feel as if he had to be an escort for me.

"I know it is not necessary, but I insist."

He held his arm out for mine. I took it and we walked the remaining distance to Valhalla. Once we reached the doors, I turned and looked up at him.

"Thank you for walking me home. I appreciate the kindness you have shown me. You have exceeded anything I would have ever expected."

A golden eyebrow raised. "What would you have expected?"

Shrugging, I grinned. "I've heard you can be quite the brute."

"Only to those who deserve it."

He cupped my cheek with one hand. Lowering his head, he brought his mouth to mine. My heart began to race as his lips dipped closer. My eyelids became heavy, closing on their own. When his lips touched mine, they were warm and gentle. My mouth opened a little and he deepened the kiss. I felt my hands grip his waist without my prompting them. It felt like something took over my body and I was just seeing and feeling with no control.

He broke the kiss, his breathing labored. He rested his forehead on mine. "I feel as if I should apologize for that, but I have no intentions of doing so. That was lovely."

I did the only thing I could since my brain wasn't fully working. I nodded.

He pulled back from me after placing a chaste kiss to my forehead. "I must be going. We aren't finished here, however. There will be discussion on this soon."

Before I could respond, he was gone. I leaned against the door, willing my breathing to slow and become regulated once again.

Sighing, I pushed off the door, so I was supporting my weight again. As I opened the door to Valhalla, a chill ran down my spine. Shivering, I glanced around. Winter was fast approaching and earlier than it was supposed to. That wasn't a good sign.

CHAPTER 7

Winter hit hard and fast. It began snowing within hours of the cold setting in. There was no sign in sight of the snowfall coming to an end. We continued to train outside, but it was harder to do with snow piling up on the fields. I supposed that it was beneficial, so we were ready for the final battle, no matter what the conditions.

After the training sessions, we would sit in the Great Hall, as close to the fireplace as we could in order to warm up. The halls of Valhalla used to be filled with laughter, but now, it was silent. There was a heaviness to the air that kept us quiet. Talking had become rare unless it was in hushed whispers.

Time seemed to run together, and I wasn't sure how long it had been since the winter set in. It didn't feel like it was ever going to end. I felt anxiety building in my chest as the thoughts of an endless winter flooded my mind.

Pacing the Great Hall, I tried to take my mind off the cold that was beyond the doors. I hadn't been able to leave Valhalla since it began to snow. My disappearing act had repercussions that I hadn't anticipated. I was barred from going anywhere off our grounds. Going to Midgard was a distant memory. I wasn't sure how long this would last. My chores of late had consisted of mucking the stalls, in addition to training the warriors.

I stopped my circuit to look out the windows. There was snow as far as the eye could see. Lightning danced across the sky, making me think of Thor yet again and the kiss we shared. My fingers came up to my lips as I stared out the window. I couldn't help but wonder what he was doing and where he was. I hadn't forgotten he told me we weren't done with that kiss.

My hand dropped, and I sighed. There was no use thinking about the past. I needed to focus on the present and preparing for whatever was coming. Taking my leave from the Great Hall, I made my way to the bunkers.

Climbing onto my cot, I stared at the ceiling while I waited for sleep to overcome me. I tossed and turned but sleep still evaded me. I knew that sleep wouldn't welcome me in its warm embrace for the night. I sat up, deciding it was best to be productive if I wasn't going to recharge my body. I was going to train some more.

***

The halls of Valhalla were silent, like they had been many nights before. The longer the darkness and cold lingered, the more it affected our people. There used to be warriors and Valkyries staying up all hours, laughing and joyous. Slowly that laughter faded. We barely spoke. The only times we were all together were during meals and training.

I found myself roaming more frequently. I was worried that we weren't going to be prepared for the battles ahead, even though we trained. If our morale was down, we would be vulnerable. I didn't know how to change it though.

Going to the stables, I decided to groom Astrid. I hoped it would settle my mind enough for me to fall asleep, if even for a short time. I waded through snow that was knee high, shivering as I went. The cold felt like it was never going to leave. It had settled in to stay.

Entering the stables, I first approached the makeshift fireplace. We had built it to help keep the animals warm after one of the horses froze to death. After rekindling the flame, I held my hands out to it to warm them. Then I turned to the stall that Astrid occupied.

"Hey, girl, I hope you aren't too cold," I murmured. I stroked her nose gently, then reached for the brush. I removed the blanket I kept on her to help maintain her body heat.

I carefully brushed her and let my mind wander. I knew there had been negotiations with Hel about the release of Baldr's soul, but I didn't believe that it was getting anywhere. She had made several agreements with us, all of which had been broken. This was a game to her, one she was winning.

My mind then drifted to a certain blond god, like it always did. I had to get him off my mind before he became the distraction that would get me killed. I couldn't have him constantly in my thoughts. I hadn't seen or heard from him since he escorted me to Valhalla after the meeting with Odin. I wondered if he was well and how he was faring in the snow and cold. As the God of Thunder, I didn't think he would like it too much. He was more of a warm weather type of god.

Resting my head on Astrid's side, I listened to the slow and steady beat of her heart. It was a reassuring sound. The methodic thump, thump, thump lured me to the illusion of safety and security. Closing my eyes, I decided to rest them for just a moment.

A crash of thunder made me jump. It wasn't a sound I'd heard in a while. Whipping around, I saw a shadowy figure standing in the doorway. He filled the door like the giant presence that he was. The shape stepped further into the stables, revealing a snow-covered Thor. He had Mjolnir in his right hand.

Studying his features, he looked like he had been to Helheim and had a rough go of it. I wanted to run into his arms, but I was afraid of the emotion and feeling behind it. I also wasn't certain of how he would react to it, so I stood there staring at him.

"I come with news." His voice was grave.

A chill ran through my body that had nothing to do with the cold, but the foreboding that washed through me. "What is it?"

"Tis best we get all the Valkyries together for this, that way I only have to say it once."

"Why did you come here first then, instead of the Great Hall?"

One eyebrow lifted, a gleam flashing through his blue eyes. "I have no idea what you are talking about."

"Seriously, Thor. You know that Brynhild doesn't visit the stables very often. She is generally in the Great Hall or her office."

He stepped closer to me, lifting my chin with a fingertip. "And who says that I was looking for Brynhild? I prefer a Valkyrie of a different style. One less regulated. One that I am aware hasn't been sleeping and spends lonely nights in the stables with her horse."

I was stunned that he knew what was going on with me. He knew my schedule too, apparently. I opened my mouth to speak, but nothing came out. I shut it and tried again. Still nothing. I was speechless that he had been keeping up with me, but I hadn't seen him.

He smiled, then his eyes grew serious. "Come, Little One. We must get the Valkyries together. This is of the upmost importance. Odin is on his way as well."

Odin was on his way to Valhalla? What had we done for that kind of honor? Maybe it wasn't an honor. Maybe we were being punished for something that he thought we had done. It wouldn't have been the first time he punished us for some conceived wrongdoing.

"We better get inside then," I said softly. I turned and covered Astrid back up, hoping she wouldn't freeze through the winter. Stoking the fire, making sure it was ablaze, I followed Thor out of the stables.

He took my arm and helped me make my way through the snow. He walked as if it wasn't there while I had to struggle to get through. We entered the Great Hall, kicking snow off our legs and boots. I walked over and began to ring the bell in the corner. Bells sounded throughout the halls of Valhalla.

The bell was only to be used during an emergency or something of great importance. I had figured Odin's pending arrival was cause for both. Brynhild was the first to make it into the Great Hall. She was scowling at me as soon as she walked through the doors.

"What is the meaning of this, Kara? Do you need to be punished yet again? You are not allowed to ring the bell. It is above your station. You know—" she cut off as soon as she realized I wasn't alone in the room.

Thor's eyebrow shot up, but not like it had earlier when he was teasing me. The look that he was giving Brynhild could only be considered condemning. He didn't say a word, but he didn't have to. I had just been berated by my superior, in front of one of our leaders, our gods. That was a serious offense in some eyes.

"Thor. M-m-my lord. I didn't know y-y-you were here." She stammered over her wording.

"I requested a meeting. Odin shall be arriving momentarily. We have matters to discuss." Thor's tone was clipped, not giving away any emotion.

She nodded, then turned and watched as the other Valkyries filed into the room. As Mist entered, the last Valkyrie to show, the great doors flew open. Odin strode in as if he were here daily. He crossed the room to stand in front of the fire. Snow fell off his boots in clumps, melting onto the floor.

When he turned to face the room, his eyes were menacing. They reminded me of the stories of the last battle with the giants. His eyes settled on Brynhild. "Is everyone present?"

After she scanned the faces in the room, she bowed her head to Odin. "Yes, Milord. All are present."

"I will get straight to the point of my being here then." He turned to address the entire room. "Loki has managed to escape his imprisonment. We are not sure how, but I suspect that someone let him out."

There was a collective gasp and murmurs started around the room. His hand shot up and the room fell silent once again.

"My guards have also notified me that Fenrir is no longer on his chain either. It stands to reason that Loki has freed Fenrir as well. To what end, we are not sure. I want you on guard at all times. Brynhild, send some warriors out to stand post with the guards. I cannot imagine anything good coming of this. Also, send some scouts out to see if they can locate where Loki has disappeared to."

"Aye, Milord." Brynhild nodded toward him. "Everything will be set up at once."

"Good." He stared at the faces in the group. "I know you have not been prepared to pick up your weapons for battle. It has been known that it could happen, which is why you train, but ladies, 'tis time that we prepare for war. Speak of this to no one. I do not want the Asgardians on edge or frightened."

I looked up at Thor, who was still and silent at my side. His eyes were hard and damning. I could see the quiet rage in them. They reminded me of a summer storm that would hit without warning. Dangerous and exciting.

Instead of feeling fear at the idea of war looming, I felt exhilaration. Anticipation flowed through me. I knew I was ready to stand up for my world and protect its people. That was what the dreams had been telling me.

"If you do locate Loki, do not attempt to apprehend him on your own. Make sure you have guards and warriors with you. He is a serpent, good at blending and striking when you least expect it." He stopped. His eyes met mine. "If you come in contact with Fenrir, just pray you make it out alive. Fenrir hasn't been free in a long time. We agreed that he was too dangerous to be allowed to roam. Now that he is out, he will be wanting blood. If possible, destroy him at the first opportunity."

I nodded in agreement with what Odin said. I wasn't sure if killing Fenrir on sight was the best idea, but I didn't know him, Odin did. If Odin and the Aesir felt he was too dangerous to live, then that was the case.

"One more thing. How are negotiations for Baldr's soul going?"

"Not well, Majesty." Mist stepped forward to approach Odin. "I fear that Hel is toying with us. We have met all of her demands, yet she refuses to let him return. We have done everything in our power except declare war with Helheim. I am currently coming up with another negotiation. An exchange. His soul for a warrior, but she hasn't responded with her terms of the deal."

"I don't like the idea of giving her one of our warriors." Thor spoke up. Odin and Mist both looked at him.

"Do you not want your brother to return to his rightful place, here in Valhalla, my son?" Odin asked, voice laced with menace and threat.

"That is not it, Father, and you know it. I fear that she will want the warrior before she hands off Baldr. What will happen then? She might choose our best warrior and then keep them both. We will be out not only my brother, but one of our best. An honored warrior."

"I will do anything to see my son home." Odin said through clenched teeth.

Thor's free hand balled into a fist. I had a feeling that a fight was about to ensue, and that wasn't something anyone needed. We needed to get along and work together.

Gently, I placed a hand on Thor's arm. "Don't. Please."

His eyes met mine. We stared at each other for several heartbeats. The rest of the room seemed to fall away, and Thor was the only thing I could see, hear, or feel. I continued to look into his eyes, wanting to look away, but afraid to at the same time. The connection felt like electricity flowing into me from him.

"Now is not the time for us to quarrel amongst ourselves. We must remain united. Discord is weakness. This is the time when we can't afford any vulnerability. Strength is what we need now." I never took my eyes off Thor.

He nodded once, then took my hand from his arm, bowing down to place a kiss on it. "You're right, little Valkyrie. We must stick together during these difficult times. Thank you for being my reason."

The world came crashing back down around us. I turned to see Mist staring at me with wide-eyed shock. There was such a silence in the room, I didn't think anyone was even breathing. I felt a flush burning my cheeks. Nodding, I attempted to step away from him, but my hand was still gripped in his. He didn't appear to be letting go.

I glanced out the window while the talk of war and strategy ensued. While I was staring outside, I saw two things that were unsettling. First, the Red Rooster was still perched in Yggdrasil. The second, the snow looked as if it was starting to melt.

CHAPTER 8

The snow melted rapidly, causing flooding in Asgard. Heat kicked in almost as if someone flipped a switch to warm it up. The light still hadn't returned, but there was cloud coverage so dark it reminded me of smoke. Flash backs of the dreams I had came to mind. Asgard in flames, smoke, destruction. There had been no sightings of Loki or Fenrir. I found that disturbing as well. He disappeared like smoke. I didn't like things happening for no reason or without some kind of sign.

I walked through a field on Midgard alongside Mist. We hadn't had much time to speak since everything had happened. We were on patrol not only for warrior souls, but also for any traces of Loki and Fenrir. Some thought that he fled to Midgard, but I didn't think he was that stupid. Midgard was Thor's territory and he had vowed to protect it. Thor took his vows seriously.

I glanced over at Mist. "Midgard is being affected as well. Look at the people. They used to be happy. There is battling, anger, and hatred here as well. It seems like evil is trying to take over."

"Evil is in the eye of the beholder," Mist murmured.

"Pardon?"

"Think about it, Kara. The perception of good and evil. How do you know we are good? Because we were told. What makes evil? Is Odin evil for fighting with the giants and almost destroying the species?"

"No, he had to." I said automatically. "He was protecting his people."

"What about the King of Jotunheim? He was protecting his people as well. Only he was trying to protect them from Odin and the Aesir. How does that make him any more evil than Odin?"

"He is. That is all there is to it." I felt like my best friend was attacking our whole belief system.

"Think, Kara." Mist stopped. She whipped around, grabbing me by the shoulders. Her violet eyes penetrated deeply into mine. Her voice lowered so I had to strain to hear her. "You need to think. Use your head. I am going to die for the Aesir and Asgard; so are you. I want you to realize the importance of it. You have your own mind. I have seen it. So has Thor, if the way he looks at you is any indication. I want you to truly see what you are devoting your life to. Consider everything. That is the part of being a Valkyrie that they don't want to teach us. You have to learn it on your own."

I thought about what she said. Surtr was Odin's sworn enemy. He had to be evil. If not, then Odin was. Or was he?

Pulling away from her, I watched two warriors battling to the death. I knew that the bigger, stronger one would win if size was all that mattered. If you didn't take heart and belief into consideration. The smaller warrior was badly beaten, but he didn't look broken. In fact, he looked determined. I had a feeling the smaller warrior would win the battle from sheer determination.

I knew that death was going to be part of this final battle we had been preparing for. Like Mist, I was willing to die for what I believed in. As the bigger warrior fell to the ground in defeat, I turned back and studied Mist. She didn't have any emotion on her face. She was just passively watching me.

Stepping back toward her, I nodded once and began walking again. "I see your point. You want me to be aware there are multiple sides to every story. Like with Loki."

"Loki?" she asked.

I nodded once. "Yes. He freed Fenrir. No one can seem to understand why he would do that, knowing how dangerous Fenrir is. It makes sense though. Loki knows the battle is coming and wants to protect his child."

She considered it for a moment. "I suppose you are right. I am relieved you understand. I didn't want to die with you at my side, not fully being aware of what we were dying for."

We finished our rounds and made our way back to the bridge to return home. When we arrived at Valhalla, I froze. Something was terribly wrong. I couldn't figure out exactly what it was though. Looking at Mist, I saw her eyes were guarded, hand on her belt next to her weapon. She was feeling it as well.

Rushing through the gates, the first thing I noticed was the stables were on fire. There were horses all over the training field. My eyes scanned the animals, looking for Astrid. She wasn't among them. Racing to the stable, I burst through the burning doors.

Embers and ashes fell from above, but I ignored the pain from the burning. I dodged as a beam fell from overhead, crashing onto the floor where I had been standing. I kicked Astrid's stall open to find her in the corner, as far from the flames as she could get.

I approached her gingerly, but swiftly, trying to reassure her as I advanced.

"It's okay, Astrid. I am going to get you out of here."

She puffed and whinnied at me. Mounting her, I leaned forward and spoke softly in her ear. "We have to get out of here swiftly or we will both perish. I know we have a lot to live for, so, shall we?"

I nudged her forward and Astrid sprang into action. She ran toward the door, trying to get us out. A beam broke and fell in front of us. Suddenly, there was a crack of thunder and the beam moved out of the way. Thor stood in the doorway of the stables. He stepped to the side so we could pass.

Once out of the stables, I dismounted and walked to him. Grabbing his hands, I examined them. They were reddened from grabbing the burning wood. Looking up into his eyes, I couldn't help but smile. "You saved us."

He gave me a half shrug. "That's my job as a hero."

I rolled my eyes and dropped his hands. Looking around, I tried to decide if anyone, Valkyrie or otherwise, was accounted for. I counted ten Valkyries, including myself. I frowned. Mist and Hild were missing.

My heart raced as I looked around, trying to find them. Mist had just been with me as we entered Valhalla. She must have had the same thought I did. Do a head count and recon. I headed toward the Great Hall; I felt the urgency of finding both of them and had to start somewhere.

I was halfway across the field when I saw Mist running from the weapons storage. She had blood on her hands and face, her eyes were wild. She ran to

Brynhild. Panting, she gasped. "Brynhild. Come quick. It's Hild. She's dead."

We followed her back toward the storage. As soon as I crossed the threshold, I could smell it. Death. Blood. The smell was overpowering. It made me want to gag, but I had to see what happened. There was blood all over the walls and floor. It looked like there was quite a battle in the room.

Hild was lying face down in a pool of blood. Cuts covered her arms, indicating that she had put up a fight. The blood had handprints in it where Mist had checked on her, from the looks of it. Thor approached her, squatting down to check to see if she was breathing. Shaking his head, he stood back up.

"Aye, she's gone. It was Loki, I'm sure of it." he said. He turned to Brynhild. "Keep the rest of the Valkyries in your sights. We need as many as we can to fight back. Be prepared for the war to come."

"Aye, Milord." Brynhild acknowledged the order then looked toward the rest of us. "You heard Thor Son of Odin. We must prepare. It looks as if Loki was trying to get our weapons. He's a sly one, he is. I will be putting warriors at these doors to ensure that no one gains entry. Eldrid and Goll, take care of this mess. I will take care of Hild's body myself. We will burn it with honors at sunset."

She approached Hild's body, lifting it like a child's, and carried it toward the Great Hall. I wasn't sure where she was taking it, but I knew that Brynhild knew what she was doing. She had survived multiple wars, which was why she was our leader. She was the eldest, smartest, and bravest of all.

Thor led the rest of us back out to the courtyard and training fields. He turned and looked at us. "Do what you must to prepare. I will be alerting the Aesir and Odin of this travesty."

Spinning his hammer, he flew off the ground and out of sight. I continued to watch until I could no longer see where he was. It was really happening. I couldn't believe it. We stood in silence for several long heartbeats while we let the events absorb.

It wasn't long after he left that we heard the noise we had been dreading. An alert. Racing to the walls that surrounded Valhalla, we entered and raced up the steps to the wall walk. My heart was thundering in my ears. There was a knot forming in the bottom of my stomach.

When I reached the top, I pushed past the others to look out into the horizon. In the distance, barely in sight, was a ship. It was no ordinary ship though. It was a ship that was the sign of destruction of Asgard. Naglfar. The ship of the dead was fast approaching.

Other than the horn sounding the alarm of the intruders, there was no other noise. Valhalla and Asgard were silent. It was as if the whole world was waiting with abated breath. I watched the ship, trying to make out any of the features on it. The sails were black and rumored to be made of the skin of the damned.

With Naglfar on the horizon, heavy clouds began to roll in with a rumbling angry thunder. I watched the dark clouds cover the sun, causing a red tint on the ground before the sun completely disappeared. It reminded me of the blood that had been all over the weapons storage. I had a feeling we would be seeing a lot more spilled blood in the days to come.

The ship was inching its way closer as we stood staring at it. My feet felt like they were glued in place, and I couldn't move. Fear washed through me, along with the realization that I wouldn't live through the fortnight.

A soft voice from behind made me jump and turn.

"Tis true then." Brynhild stared out toward the ocean. "Our biggest fear has come to pass. We are facing Ragnarök. Come. Let us say goodbye to our sister, then prepare for the war of a lifetime."

With that, everyone followed Brynhild down the stairs and out of Valhalla. We stood at the edge of the ocean. A small wooden boat with Hild's body, all wrapped in cloth, was on the edge of the water.

I watched with a lump in my throat as Brynhild picked up a torch, setting an edge of the cloth on fire. She shoved the small craft into the water and we watched in silence as the flames engulfed the body. Smoke filled the air. It smelled like cooking meat and burnt hair.

"We say goodbye to our sister, Hild. She was by my side many years, her life ended before her destiny was fulfilled." Brynhild turned to face us, her back to the burning body out in the ocean. "She was born a Viking in her first life, then came to us. Now she gets to rest in honor among her blood. She was a Valkyrie through and through. Pure of heart. She believed in our cause and purpose. We will fight this battle, give our lives. Not only because it is our duty, but also to show Hild she did not die in vain. Every death of the enemy will be a gift to her. We will show Odin and the rest of the Aesir that they made the right choice in choosing us. We are more than pretty faces. We will kick arse and protect Asgard."

Her speech took my breath away. Our home, our lives as we knew it were about to change. Nothing would be the same after this. I watched Hild's body drifting in the ocean, like a beacon for the gods to find her soul to take her home.

My eyes drifted over to the ship that was getting larger in the distance. I could make out two figures standing at the helm. I wasn't sure how I knew, but I knew one of them would be Loki. So that meant the other was Hel. It felt as if hellhounds were nipping at our heels as we stood here vulnerable.

"Let us get dressed for war." Brynhild's eyes met mine. "Ragnarök has arrived."

CHAPTER 9

I helped Mist into her armor as we armed ourselves. I knew that Loki and his army would be here before the dawn. We had little time left of the quiet before chaos ensued. Once her armor was on, I picked up a sword and slid it into the sheath on my hip. I loaded a quiver with arrows and grabbed a bow. I was going to be as prepared as I could for the end.

"I thought about what you said," I told her suddenly.

Mist looked up, eyes meeting mine. "And?"

"I can see where you are coming from, but you have to look at it from another aspect as well."

"Which aspect is that?"

"What is better for the people. I don't mean our people or their people. I mean all the people. The Asgardians, the giants, the mortals. I believe in doing what's right and best for everyone."

She hugged me, squeezing me tightly. I returned the hug, confused by the sudden outburst of emotion. Mist was always controlled. It wasn't like her to show affection like that.

She smiled as she pulled away from me. "Kara, you are special. I am so glad you understand that."

She turned and began preparing her weapons as well. Maybe she just needed to express it before we died. It would make sense. I wasn't sure what was

71

going on, but my stomach was telling me something was amiss. I shook myself mentally and tried to focus on the battles that were coming to a head.

The door opened suddenly. Turning, I saw Thor standing there. His eyes were clouded, face grim. He walked into the room, shutting the door gently behind him. He was dressed in his armor, along with his cape and helmet. He looked majestic and dangerous.

My mouth dried out as I stared at him. He was stunning. My heart sped up. A part of me wanted to run into his arms, but I just stood there. Waiting.

"I need to speak to you alone, little Valkyrie." His voice left no room for argument.

Mist silently dismissed herself to give us some privacy.

"What is it, Milord?" I asked while tightening my belt. I wanted to make sure my weapons stayed secure.

He stepped closer, forcing me to look up to see into his eyes. "There are things that need to be said now. We may not have time otherwise."

"I'm listening."

"Kara, I want you by my side after the battle is over."

I frowned. "I will always stand beside you, Majesty."

"That isn't what I mean." He took his finger, gently lifting my chin up higher so my head was tilted back, neck exposed. I was in a vulnerable position like that, but I felt safe.

"Then what do you mean?"

"I want you. With me." He leaned closer, stopping when his mouth was mere inches from mine. "I want to be with you. I want you to be mine."

My heart fluttered, stomach flipped. I felt excitement and fear at his statement. "I can't be with you in that sense without becoming a used lady."

His eyes hardened. "I want you to be my wife. I can't get you out of my head. You have been all I think of since I saw you on the cliff. You were alone, concerned. You have touched something deep within me. If you say yes, then you will never have to worry about becoming a whore. You would become queen when I take the throne after Odin. You will be my only wife. You are the only woman I want."

I stared at him, unsure of how to answer. He was offering me the world. All I had to do was say yes. He was all that I had thought of as well, but I didn't tell him. Fear ran through me. I didn't expect to survive the war, so none of this made any sense.

"Thor, we probably won't live past the war." My voice wavered as I spoke.

"Are you refusing my hand?" His eyes were wide; he looked genuinely hurt.

"No. I am not refusing. I am just putting it into perspective. You are truly asking for my hand hours before we start the battle that will end Asgard?"

"Aye. I know it sounds crazy, but is there truly a better time to do this?"

I took a deep breath and let it out slowly. "I will marry you. However, I wish to wait until after the war. We needn't rush things. If we were to wed before the battles begin, you would be distracted by my presence. I am a Valkyrie, and I will do my job no matter what."

"I expect nothing less from you. You drive a hard bargain, Kara. We will be wed on sunset the day after the battles end, and we ring victorious."

His mouth came down on mine. My arms wrapped around his neck of their own accord. My knees felt like they were melting and couldn't hold me up. His arms went around my waist as my legs gave out on me. I felt the kiss to my core.

The sound of Heimdall's horn alerting us of the impending intruders broke the spell, bringing me back to reality. Thor steadied me on my feet, then placed a kiss on my knuckles.

"Let us show them that coming after us was the wrong choice. Shall we, my love?"

I smiled at him. "We shall."

"That's my girl."

We walked out, joining the rest of the Valkyries and warriors in the courtyard. Brynhild was standing atop the stairs. She was dressed for battle, as was everyone in attendance. She barked commands out, which were followed without hesitation.

"Valkyries! Warriors! The time has come to prove your worth. This is what we have dedicated our lives to. We will fight to the death and drive Hel and Loki from Asgard. They will regret ever stepping foot on our land and harming our people." Her eyes scanned the crowd as she spoke. Her voice rang clearly through the courtyard. "For Asgard!"

"For Asgard! For Asgard! For Asgard!" warriors and Valkyries alike chanted.

"For Baldr," Thor said softly.

My heart ached for him. I hadn't thought much about the fact that his brother had died during all of this, and he was still mourning the loss. I wanted to wrap my arms around him and tell him it was going to be okay. Instead, I reached out and grabbed his hand. He looked down at me with a gentle smile on his face.

Horses neighed and stomped the ground anxiously. The horn in the distance continued to sound. Weapons and armor clinked as warriors moved around, ready.

The noise all screamed war. I should have been afraid, yet I wasn't. I was excited. I felt the adrenaline rushing through my veins. I was ready to kill and protect my home.

I mounted Astrid and followed the others toward the doors. They opened on their own as we approached. I had never seen all five hundred forty doors open at the same time before. We passed through the doors as one unit into Asgard.

The sight was heart wrenching. The warriors from Helheim were everywhere. Slaying people they passed. There were men, women, and children lying lifelessly on the ground. My heart hurt for those who had perished.

The Aesir were on the battlefield, which used to contain the crops that fed the Asgardians. The crops had been trampled underfoot by the troops and warriors. The ground was littered with the bodies of the fallen.

The soldiers from Helheim fought with all their might and they were ruthless. I watched as one snuck up behind a palace guard and slit his throat. Blood squirted from his neck in an arc. The guard's eyes bulged, his mouth opened and closed before he collapsed to the ground.

I sent a quick prayer up that I would survive the first battle, then urged Astrid forward. Valkyries and warriors alike cried a battle cry as they plunged into the fighting. Swords clanged, screams sounded as the fighting commenced.

I directed my attention to the battle ahead of me and what I needed to do. I let all the sounds fade out as I focused on the conflict ahead. I became one with Astrid and my sword. My arm swung seamlessly down, decapitating the first soldier that I came upon. Blood sprayed me as his head rolled off his shoulders.

I became so absorbed in the battle, I wasn't sure how much time had passed before I pulled myself from my head. I was shocked and disheartened to see that we had lost as many warriors as we had. My heart was heavy and aching from the losses.

Thor approached me, putting a gentle hand on Astrid's neck. I looked down at him, suddenly weary. It felt like all my energy had been sucked out of me during the battle.

"You did very well today, Kara." he said softly. "We won this fight."

"Thank you. We won this battle, but at what cost? How much did we lose today than we had to begin with? Is the loss of life that insignificant?"

"It is natural to feel the way you are after your first battle. The death and bloodshed are hard to deal with, however you will adjust quick enough. By the end of this war, you will not think twice about what was sacrificed until the battle is finished. You will learn to push it from your mind."

"That is a sad way to live. You shouldn't forget about the loss or how we gain our successes. Those who perish should be remembered and honored."

"They are. Right here." Thor reached up and gently tapped my chest above my heart. "Every life lost will stick with you forever, but you can't let it keep you down."

I nodded. He was right. I would hold the fallen inside me for the rest of my life.

"Come on, I have a surprise for you. Something to take your mind off of the fighting today."

I frowned as I looked down at him. "I doubt you can take my mind off the death. Nothing will ease the pain from my mind."

He led Astrid off the field. We headed toward the palace, then veered off to a small path. The trail was dark and overgrown. At the end of the pathway was a cottage. Lights flickered in the window from the candlelight.

Thor tied Astrid to a post, then lifted me off her by my waist. As he set my feet down on the ground, I frowned. "What are you up to?"

"You will see," Thor said, gripping my hand. He led me into the cottage.

Once inside, I was surprised and confused by the scene before me. Odin and Mist stood in the far corner of the room, talking softly. There were candles all over, casting a glow bright enough to see, but not enough to completely light the room.

"Does someone wish to tell me what is going on now?" I could hear the sharpness in my own voice, but there was nothing I could do about it. I was getting tired of the secret and wanted to know what was happening.

"I was speaking with my father. We decided that it would be best if you and I go ahead and wed, just us. After the war, we will celebrate and have a public union." Thor said, leading me further into the room, closer to Odin.

"I don't know what to say," I mumbled. My mind was scrambling to catch up with the events of the day.

"Say yes."

Looking up into his eyes, I could see the candle from behind me flickering there. The look was intense and pleading. I did the only thing I could. "Yes."

His smile melted my heart and my knees. In that moment, I knew that I was in trouble. I was also aware that I would go through Helheim for him. He led me up to where Odin was standing. We stopped directly in front of Odin.

"Are ye sure this is what ye want?" Odin asked.

"Aye," Thor answered.

"Aye," I responded. I didn't look toward Odin. I couldn't pull my eyes away from Thor.

As the ceremony proceeded, I felt a calm settle over me. It was a peaceful feeling that I shouldn't have felt during the time of great conflict. I was trapped in Thor's eyes, not even aware when I repeated the vows that bound us together for the rest of eternity.

When the ceremony ended, Thor gently placed his lips on mine to seal the vows. As he pulled away, I felt like I could feel the connection still. I couldn't believe it. I was officially attached to Thor for the rest of my days, no matter how long that would be.

CHAPTER 10

It felt like my head was spinning. I was still in a daze from the events of the day. Thor took me by the waist and danced around the floor with me. Instead of music playing, he hummed a melody in my ear. I was floating across the floor with him. There wasn't a time that I could remember where I was happier. Nothing was going to be able to destroy my happiness.

When the dance ended, Thor pressed his lips gently against mine. "I can't wait to get you alone, wife."

I smiled. "Wife, I like that."

A horn sounded in the distance, which caused us to step apart. I groaned inwardly. What in the fresh Helheim was this? I wouldn't have to wait long to find out.

Screams began to float across the air, along with a distinct howl. I looked at Thor, then Odin, to see the color drain from their faces. It couldn't be what I thought. I silently prayed I was wrong.

"We must go." Odin said, a sad expression on his face.

Glancing at Mist, I looked back toward them. "Is that-"

"Fenrir." Thor supplied when I cut myself off.

If Fenrir was here, then we were doomed. The Aesir had feared him so much they had tricked him onto an island and chained him with an unbreakable chain, so he couldn't come back to Asgard and wreak havoc. Now he was free, thanks to Loki. Rumor was he was twice the size of a giant, but he hadn't been seen in years.

"Odin's right. We must go and stop Fenrir from slaying everything in sight." Mist was already collecting her weapons, which she had set down for the ceremony.

Once we were suited up again, we made our way outside. Thor stopped me beside Astrid. "I'm sorry our union was short lived. We will make up for it later."

I nodded before he kissed me once more on the lips.

"Let's go to battle." I smiled through the tears that were building behind my eyes. I wasn't sure why I was about to cry, but I wasn't going to show any weakness. Battle was what I was made for. It was all I knew, so I would do what I was born to do.

Thor took flight as Mist and I followed on our horses. As Astrid took to the sky, I gripped her mane a little tighter. Adrenaline rushed through my veins; the thought of the battle excited my blood. I was Valkyrie, first and foremost.

The scene ahead was heart-stopping. There were bodies strewn about as the giant wolf tossed Asgardians around like ragdolls. I felt frozen in horror from the scene I was witnessing. The thunder and lightning shook me out of my shocked state.

I watched as Thor flew into the midst of the chaos, attacking Fenrir with enough fervor to make the monster falter. He took two steps back, then snarled at Thor. His incisors glistened in the light; saliva mixed with blood dripping off the points of his fangs.

Guiding Astrid to the ground, I ran into the throes of battle. Mist was by my side as we fought our way into the middle of the chaos. Thor landed on my other side and turned me toward him.

"Do what you can to evacuate and take down Fenrir. I'm going after Loki. I spotted him due north."

I nodded and watched him take flight again. Looking over at Mist, I smiled. "Here goes nothing. Let's kick ass."

During the fighting, I lost track of Mist as I made my way to Fenrir. My heart pounded in my ears and fear ran down my back, but I wasn't going to back down. I had to do this. For myself. For Asgard. For Thor.

Each swing of my sword into one of the bodies of the army Loki brought with him, made a sickening thud before the screams ensued. I found it easier to try to decapitate them so I wouldn't have to hear the cries of agony.

One of the soldiers that Loki had unleashed had a woman trapped in his arms. It looked like he was chewing on her neck. I whipped out my bow and an arrow. Aiming, I took the shot. The arrow cut through the air, hitting its mark. It went through the temple of the monster attacking the woman. The woman pushed him away and ran in the opposite direction.

Suddenly, I came face to face with one of the warriors that had not been chosen for Valhalla. I recognized him from the battlefields on Midgard. He had been a dark soul, not worthy of joining us. He had cheated and fought unjustly. The smile he gave me sent chills down my spine. I didn't know why, but I thought he recognized me as well.

"This shall be fun," he snarled at me.

"Agreed." I took my stance, watching him warily. If he could overpower me, I was done for. The warrior was twice my size. I only hoped that I had more training and agility than he did.

We circled each other slowly, my eyes never leaving the darkness of his. I tried to assess any weaknesses he might have, but I was afraid to look away for an instant. All my training had taught me that I had to watch for signs of attack.

I dodged his first attack by a hair. I almost hadn't seen his fist coming. I took my sword and swung it at him. He caught it by the blade and yanked it out of my hands. Tossing it, he smiled again. That smile would put an average warrior off guard, but not me. Valkyries were made of sterner stuff than that. I dropped to the ground, sweeping his legs out from under him. As he hit the dirt, he grabbed me.

Rolling around on the ground with him, we exchanged punches. The blows to my head were making my ears ring. Then what I feared most happened. The warrior got the upper hand. He managed to climb on top of me, wrap his meaty hands around my throat, and begin to choke the life out of me.

Reaching down to my boot, my fingers wrapped around the hilt of the dagger I kept there. It had been my mother's dagger. I didn't know much about my parents, but it had been the one possession of hers I had been allotted. Releasing the dagger from its sheath, I took it and plunged it into the warrior's eye. When it resisted, I pushed harder until I felt the bone crack and give.

The warrior howled in pain and released my neck. As he scrambled away from me, I jerked the dagger from his eye socket and shoved it into his chest. He stared at me in shock as blood and fluid from his eyeball ran down his face. Realizing he lost to a woman, he staggered backwards, then faceplanted on the ground. A red pool of blood began to spread around him.

Standing, I wiped the blade of my dagger off on the dead warrior's shirt, then replaced it in its sheath. I retrieved my sword and turned to see Fenrir turning in my direction.

Fenrir's attention landed on me, and he licked his lips. As he attacked, I jumped back and swung my sword. In that moment, I knew what death looked like. I knew that I wasn't going to survive the battle with the huge wolf. He would swallow me whole or leave me to die in pieces.

Knocking me over with a paw, he stood on me, bringing his muzzle down to sniff me. As the hot air escaped his nostrils, I fought the shiver of fear. I couldn't let him smell how afraid I was. His mouth opened, and he made a move for my throat.

My eyes squeezed shut out of reaction. I didn't want to see the razor-sharp teeth coming to end my life. The wolf's weight suddenly lifted off me. Being able to breathe again, I inhaled deeply, filling my oxygen-deprived lungs with air. I opened my eyes and sat straight up, looking around to see what happened.

Odin had the wolf backed against a building. He swung his sword at the wolf, slicing Fenrir's throat. Blood sprayed all over Odin, coloring him red. The wolf howled in pain, lunging at the god. His strong jaw locked onto Odin's shoulder, throwing him several feet. I watched in horror as the battle between the two continued until the wolf's steps faltered and Fenrir finally collapsed to the ground.

Odin staggered a couple steps before dropping to his knees. I let go of my sword and sprinted to his side.

"All-Father, are you alright? You saved my life. Why? I am supposed to die for you."

He smiled, blood coming out of the corner of his mouth. "Kara, child, you have done something I have never seen anyone, mortal or otherwise, do. I have seen you bring the light back into my son, Thor's, eyes. You are destined for greater things than dying here this day."

He coughed, blood and spittle spraying from his mouth.

"I am only a Valkyrie. My job was to die protecting you. I have failed." I could feel the tears burning in the back of my eyes.

"You have only failed in one thing, Kara. Knowing your true purpose. Yes, Valkyries are meant to fight, protect Asgard, and die. But some have greater purpose." He coughed, then gasped for air. I could hear the rattle in his chest of his lungs filling with blood. "You will learn your purpose soon, daughter."

I cradled Odin in my arms as he struggled to live for the last minutes of his existence. When he took his last breath, a tear escaped from the corner of his eye. A quiet filled the air. The loss of our All-Father hanging above us.

Standing slowly, I walked back to my sword and picked it up. Odin's words were echoing through my head. Glancing down, I saw that I wore his blood. It seemed fitting that I dove back into battle with Odin's blood, mingling with the blood of our enemies, on me.

It was up to me now. I had to stand up and do what needed to be done. I couldn't let Asgard be destroyed. It was imperative for me to survive the battle and find my true purpose. If Odin believed that I wasn't meant to die in battle, then I wasn't. He thought I had a greater purpose. It likely had to do with Thor.

As I gathered my resolve, I looked up to see Surtr. He was here to destroy Asgard. I knew then that we were fighting a losing battle. We had to save the Asgardians. The land was just that, land. It didn't seem as important as the lives that were at risk. I saw Brynhild riding toward soldiers.

"Evacuate everyone to the Rainbow Bridge! We have to get them out of here!" I shouted. She looked in my direction and gave me a nod. She turned her horse then headed out to help evacuate.

I ran toward the last place I had seen Thor. The sight made my heart stop. Loki had Thor down on the ground. Thor's hammer was several feet away, and he was struggling to get to his feet. Loki's spear was pressed against Thor's chest. He raised it and shoved it into Thor. I screamed then jumped and crashed against Loki.

He stumbled back a couple steps before he knocked me to the ground. Holding out his hand, a sword materialized instantaneously into it. He smiled down at me. "Now you can watch your beloved Thor die before I kill you."

He swung the sword down in an attempt to decapitate Thor, but before the sword touched him, a hand shot out and grabbed his arm. Mist yanked him back a couple steps. She stood in front of him, placing her hands on his face.

"No," she whispered. "Please. For me."

"For you." He kissed her gently on the lips.

I was shocked by the fact that Loki listened to her. Then it dawned on me. Loki loved her. Mist had just saved Thor's life.

Chapter 11

Loki vanished before my eyes. His magic still amazed me. I knew incredible things were possible, but to see it out in the open like that always messed with me. Once all traces of Loki were gone, Mist helped me to my feet. Flames were starting to surround us.

"We have to get going." Mist started to pull me toward the Rainbow Bridge.

"Wait! I can't leave Thor behind. Help me get him," I rushed over to his side. He was still breathing, but he hadn't opened his eyes or moved since he was stabbed.

I studied the spear. It was lodged in his chest, but it appeared to have missed his heart. I grabbed it and yanked, hoping that I didn't kill him. I ripped the bottom of his cape and bunched it against the wound. Then I ripped another strip and had Mist hold him up while I wound it around his chest to hold the first piece in place.

Mist helped me lift him and we half carried, half dragged him through the streets of Asgard toward the bridge. We had to get him and the rest of the people out of here before everyone was destroyed. As we approached the bridge, we were stalled by the crowds of people swarming around and panicking.

"What's going on?" I shouted over the roar of the people.

"Heimdall has been injured and there is no one operating the bridge," someone from ahead shouted back.

Heimdall was injured? Panic began to rise in my chest because he was the only one who knew how to work the bridge. If he wasn't controlling it, everyone would die for sure. I looked at Mist. Her eyes were wide, and she was slightly pale.

I understood her fear. Heimdall was the only one that had controlled the Rainbow Bridge for eons. I wasn't sure if anyone else was trained on how to open the bridge. I took a deep breath and readjusted my grip on Thor.

"Let's go. We will figure it out." I started forward, not giving Mist a chance to argue or change my mind. We were going to open the bridge and save the people. That was our purpose. To save the Asgardians.

Making our way through the sea of people was a daunting task, especially carrying Thor's dead weight. He needed medical assistance and wouldn't be able to get it until everyone was safe. When we reached the Bi-Frost, I looked at Mist.

"Let's put him down over here and I'll run the Bi-Frost."

She swallowed hard. "Do you know what you are doing?"

After giving a half shrug, I ran to the far wall where Heimdall was lying. Blood was gushing from his chest. I knelt beside him, shaking him gently. I needed him awake.

"Heimdall. Heimdall. Please, I need your help." I whispered softly. "I need to know how to run the Bi-Frost. We have to save the people."

His eyes opened. His stare was intense. I could see the pain around the edges of his eyes, but he didn't cry out. He simply nodded, he reached out with a shaking hand, to hand me his staff. When he spoke, his voice was barely above a whisper. "Use the staff. It knows what to do, just stand at the helm and turn it."

I nodded. "Thank you, friend. We will send you down also."

"Do not worry about me. Just get the others to safety, Valkyrie."

I stood and approached what he called the helm. It looked like a large podium. As I stepped up to it, there was a light emanating from the floor. There was an indentation where the base of the staff belonged. I was unsure of how I knew that, but I did.

I set the base into the indentation. There was a whirling sound, and the room began to shift. There was a light that shot out of the Bi-Frost, showing the rest of the Rainbow Bridge. It was the part of the bridge that sent you to other worlds and realms. As a Valkyrie, I had no need for it before, so it was fascinating.

"Mist, start bringing them in. I don't want to keep the bridge open too long. We need to hurry."

I glanced toward the window to see the palace covered in flames. The fire lit up the sky and clouds. It was terrifyingly beautiful. The sound of the scared people turned my attention from Surtr destroying Asgard.

Mist was directing them to the opening. Before anyone stepped through, I felt compelled to say something to them. "People of Asgard. When you step into the bridge, you will be sent to a new land. It is scary, but we will have Valkyries waiting on the other side. They will lead you to your new home. Be safe."

The people began to go through the bridge in droves. As the crowd began to dwindle, the flames and destruction came closer. Panic was beginning to rise, and the crowd became more aggressive. There were several Valkyries that were helping with the transport and keeping the people under control. Fear was causing them to become more reckless.

Men, women, and children were shoving each other around, trying to get to the bridge. I watched as a Valkyrie broke up one fight between two men. She yanked the aggressor out of the crowd by his hair. I could hear her threatening tone as she told him he would be the last to exit through the bridge.

When the last person crossed the bridge, just the Valkyries, Heimdall, and Thor were left in the Bi-Frost. Looking around the room, I felt a sense of sadness wash over me. I didn't know what was going to happen next, but I feared that it would be devastating to all in the room.

There was an explosion that caused everyone to rush to the window. What I saw saddened and enraged me. Valhalla was now in flames. It was supposed to be the one place that was safe from all harm, yet Surtr had destroyed it in the blink of an eye.

Turning, I studied the faces in the room. They were drawn and shocked. I could feel the heartache spread through the space. We lost our home.

"It is time. We must go." I nodded my head toward the bridge.

One by one, the Valkyries disappeared through the bridge. Finally, there were three of us left, Mist, Brynhild, and myself. We still needed to get Thor through the bridge. There was just one problem.

"How are we going to close the bridge?" I asked the question that lingered in the air. "Someone has to stay behind and close it, but we have to get Thor through as well. Under no circumstances is the God of Thunder to be left here. He must be cared for."

As I was speaking, I knew that I would be the one to close the bridge. I had to trust Thor's life in the hands of my sisters. I just hoped he wouldn't be mad at me for what I had to do.

"Brynhild, I want you to go with him. Please, get him aid as soon as you cross. He needs medical attention."

"Aye, Kara. I am proud of the Valkyrie that you have become. You have become the woman, the warrior you were meant to be." She embraced me, then studied my eyes. "You should say good-bye to your husband. I know that you are wed and how much this hurts you."

I nodded once then knelt beside Thor. "My love. Please forgive me. I have to stay behind. We cannot let Surtr enter the bridge and make his way to the other worlds. He has to stay here. If he follows us, he will destroy Midgard as well. You know we can't let that happen. Just know that the Asgardians are safe. I love you."

Tears filled my eyes as I helped Brynhild hoist him up onto her shoulders. I blinked rapidly, trying to work the tears back. I couldn't let myself give into weakness. I still had to close the bridge. Once they disappeared, I turned to Mist.

"Your turn."

There was a rumbling, and the Bi-Frost began to shake. Once the shaking came to a stop, I looked out to see the bridge leading to the Bi-Frost was on fire and beginning to crumble. Steam rose up from the rapidly evaporating water.

"Mist, you have to go now!" I shouted as I ran toward her.

She wrapped her arms around me in a tight embrace. She spoke so softly that I could barely hear her. "I'm sorry."

Pulling back, I frowned. "For what?"

Suddenly Loki appeared at her side. She shoved me backward. I stumbled, trying to regain my footing, but instead I fell into the bridge. I kept my eyes on her as I fell into the abyss. Flames erupted around her and Loki. He grabbed her hand and twisted the staff, closing the bridge.

When I landed on the ground, I coughed and gasped from the wind being knocked out of me. I sat up, anger and betrayal washing over me. I had been betrayed by my best friend. Mist was on Loki's side the entire time. I didn't know what I was going to do. I needed answers. Why would she take the wrong side? Against us. It didn't make sense.

I screamed and punched the ground beside me. I had been an idiot. The one person I trusted had turned on me. I punched the ground until my knuckles bled. Then I cried until my eyes burned and I couldn't cry anymore.

Standing up, I dusted myself off and started out on foot. I had to find Mist. I needed answers. Answers that only she could provide.

My heart ached from wanting to go find Thor, but Mist first.

CHAPTER 12

I had no idea where in Midgard I ended up. I just knew that I had to start moving. My heart warred with my head about where I needed to go. My heart screamed that I go find Thor. My mind said that I needed to find Mist.

Mist should have died in Asgard, but I had a feeling she survived. She had betrayed everything we believed in. She chose evil over her sisters. As I began walking, I contemplated what it meant. Conversations ran through my head. I tried to find any clues that she had been betraying us from the beginning.

All I could think about was how supportive she had always been. I loved her. She was more than my sister Valkyrie. She was my best friend, my soul mate. She was the other half of me. She wasn't my soulmate in a romantic aspect, but a spiritual one. We melded together.

My memories only made the betrayal hurt worse. I felt the tears burning in the back of my eyes and decided that I would let them go since I was alone. Most saw crying as weakness. I now felt that it was a sign of strength. Releasing the frustrations cleared one's head and brought peace of mind.

I allowed the tears to dry on my face without wiping them off. I could only imagine how I looked, covered in blood and dirt. I wasn't going to blend in this place very well. However, things had changed so much in the past few months, maybe I wouldn't stand out too much.

I wasn't sure how long I had been walking, but my feet began to ache. Stopping, I surveyed the land. There wasn't much to it. Dead. It looked like the Midgardians were killing the land, along with each other. I knew there had been issues here, and war, but I hadn't realized to what extent.

If the fighting didn't stop, then everything would surely die. They had to stop. This was the last place we could go. I sighed; it seemed like we were in an endless cycle of mass destruction. Something had to be done before everything was destroyed.

During the walk, I decided that I would do everything in my power to make sure this world was preserved. With a new purpose, I strode across the fields of dead grass and bodies. There were scorch marks on the ground where things had been burned.

The scorch marks reminded me of the destruction of Asgard. My heart was heavy with the weight of what happened. I tried to shake the feeling. It wasn't going to help anything to be overcome with sadness. I had many things to do.

As the sun was beginning to set, I happened upon the first signs of civilization since arriving. There were cloth shelters put up in a small gathering. A fire blazed in the middle of it. It looked welcoming. There was an aroma of cooking meat in the air. My stomach growled, reminding me I hadn't eaten in a while.

Approaching the campsite with caution, I was unsure that I would be welcomed with the group. The sounds of talking died down as I came closer. I held my hands up in an unarmed gesture, hoping they wouldn't attack.

I swallowed, trying to wet my dry throat before I spoke. I hadn't had water since coming here either. "I mean you no harm. I am just looking for shelter for the night and possibly some sustenance."

My voice was soft and foreign sounding. I didn't even recognize it. A big man approached me, studying me carefully.

"What are you? You aren't human, fae, demon, shifter, or witch." There was accusation in his tone.

He appeared to be unarmed, but I had a feeling he was more dangerous than he seemed. After a quick evaluation, I decided to go along with it and stayed in a relaxed position.

"Valkyrie." I held my head high.

"Valkyrie?" he repeated with a frown. I wasn't sure if he had even heard of us before. "They exist? I've never met one before. Didn't realize they exist."

I cocked an eyebrow. "Well, we do."

"I see that. Why are you out roaming the land? It's dangerous out here nowadays."

"It's a long story. I'm weary and parched. Please, Sir."

He stepped out of the way and allowed me passage into the camp. As I crossed the boundary of camp, I had a rush of power wash up my arms. Someone powerful had done a spell. The hair on the back of my neck stood up, putting me on alert for danger.

The camp was bigger than I initially thought. Walking to the center, I was shown to a log where I could perch and rest my legs. When I finally sat, my legs tingled and throbbed from the nonstop walking. Absently, I rubbed the muscle to help relax it.

A young woman brought me a wooden bowl filled with an assortment of berries. "Eat these while we cook up the meat. They will hold you over. Cameron will be back with more water shortly."

My first bite into a berry sent a burst of sweet goodness into my mouth and throat. It felt like I had never had anything so wonderful in my life. Next thing I knew, I was shoveling them into my mouth. I had to force myself to slow down and savor the food.

Shortly after I finished the fruit, I was brought a serving of meat and a pouch of water. I drank half the water in a couple of swallows. Next thing I knew, I had half the meat eaten without tasting it. When I looked around, I noticed I was being stared at by everyone sitting around the campfire.

Wiping my mouth with the back of my hand, I smiled sheepishly. "I apologize for being rude. I didn't realize how hungry I was."

The man that had questioned me smiled and nodded. "It's quite alright. I'm ready to hear your story now. My name is Bane, since I forgot to introduce myself earlier, Valkyrie."

"I'm Kara." Licking my lips, I debated on how much I needed to tell them. I didn't know who, or what they were, so telling them may not have been wise. However, they were being hospitable to a strange being. "I am here because we had to evacuate Asgard."

"Who had to evacuate Asgard?" Bane leaned forward, bracing his elbows on his knees. His eyes were on me intensely.

"Everyone." I swallowed. "I apologize, it is a little hard to speak about."

"When will it be safe to return?"

I studied Bane while analyzing his question. He didn't look like he was planning something devious. The question seemed genuine and full of concern.

"I don't think it will be. My people have had to seek refuge and I am trying to find answers."

"What kind of answers?"

"Answers to my questions. That is all I will say about it."

Silence filled the air as we sat around the fire. I watched it crackle and pop, mesmerized by the dance of the flames. My mind drifted to Thor. My husband. I had no idea if he survived the trip. I hadn't even been married to him a full day before we were separated.

Mentally shaking myself, I made eye contact with Bane. "What is happening here? I know war is big on Midgard, yet this is more than it has ever been."

Bane's head shot back toward me. I supposed my question caught him off guard. "You don't know?"

I shook my head no.

"The demons have overtaken the earth and we have been trying to fight them back. It hasn't been easy, and a lot of people and beings have died." He looked over my shoulder, my guess was to stare into the darkness of the woods. "They say this is the end of the world. The apocalypse has finally hit after eons of talking about it. I don't know if I would say that, but it's bad. Things will never be the same."

It was fascinating. Both Midgard and Asgard were going through very similar, almost identical, situations. I wondered if theirs was prophesized as well. It couldn't have been a coincidence that both worlds had the same issues.

After Bane described what had been going on, I knew what I had to do. I was going to help push the demons back, on my way to find Mist. I couldn't forget my mission entirely, but I also knew that I couldn't do nothing. I was born to help.

"In the morn, I must be on my way, but know this: I will help in any way that I can." I placed my hand over my heart.

"Thank you," Bane gave me a nod. "The prince of the fae will be here when the sun begins to rise, to go over battle plans. This is our rendezvous point this round. Get some rest, Kara. You never know when you'll need to fight."

The woman that brought me the bowl of fruit earlier appeared at my side. "If you come with me, I will show you where you can sleep. I hope you don't mind sharing a tent with me. Space is limited."

"Anything is fine, thank you." I stood and followed her to the hut she called a tent.

Holding the flap open for me, she allowed me entrance first. Once inside, she ducked in and lit a strange contraption. I studied it, never having seen one before. It had a base full of a red liquid and some kind of cloth that held the fire in a soft glow.

"What is that thing?"

She giggled. "It's a kerosene lamp. It's an antique from the olden days. With things the way they are, electricity is rare, so these lamps are making a comeback."

"What's electricity?" This lady wasn't making any sense.

"It's how we light, heat, cook, and everything else the humans want to do. It's a human thing." She looked down at the lamp and shrugged. "We have to learn to adapt if we are to survive."

"That is where you are wrong. You don't have to adapt; you have to fight."

"I wish it was that easy. But, Kara, we don't stand a chance against the demons. If the gods were to intervene, then maybe we could."

I cocked my head at her. "Why wouldn't they?"

She sighed. It was a heavy oppressive sound. "They think the humans brought this on themselves. The rest of us have to deal and survive. Yes, the demons could wipe out the humans in one clean sweep, but the rest of the communities won't let that happen. We have to have balance."

"Agreed. Maybe someone could speak with the gods." My mind flashed back to Odin and how hardheaded he was when the signs of Ragnarök began to appear. Gods were fickle.

"Who could we get to talk to them? Who could make them understand?"

"I will." I settled down on the ground. "I've dealt with worse. Can I have your name?"

"Christine."

I nodded. "Nice to meet you, Christine. Is this rude, or can I ask what you are? I know you aren't human by the way you speak about them."

She looked down at her hands for a moment before speaking.

"I try not to speak harshly of the humans. I know they are ignorant beings; sometimes it slips." Looking up at me, her eyes were an eerie shade of blue that seemed to be glowing. "I'm an oracle."

I had heard of oracles. They were powerful seers and magic holders. There had been talk of oracles at Valhalla. They were to be revered and respected.

We talked a little bit more before settling down for the night. She turned the light down on the lamp. I listened to her as she drifted off to sleep. Her breathing had changed dramatically. It slowed and deepened, the way only those in a deep sleep could breathe.

Sleep evaded me. I listened to the sounds of nature and the campsite. I was beginning to believe that they didn't truly sleep here. There was a howl in the distance that cemented my thoughts. Something was awake still. It was vastly different from Valhalla.

When we went to sleep in Valhalla, all was quiet and still. It seemed when the lights went out, everything went to sleep. The only ones awake when everyone was asleep were those who were chosen for the nightly patrol. Even they didn't make a sound. They moved silently through the night, making sure all stayed as it was supposed to.

The thoughts of home made my stomach hurt. I closed my eyes, trying to shift my thinking to something less painful. However, the events of the past few days weighed heavily on my mind. I wondered where Thor was and if he was okay. My heart ached for him. I hoped he was alright.

The thought of Mist and her betrayal was like a slap across the face. The pain washed through me. It was something I would have to put aside until I was able to deal with it. Now wasn't the time. I did my best to clear my mind and spent the rest of the evening staring at the roof of the tent.

The darkness began to fade as the day broke. As quietly as possible, I climbed out of the tent and began to wander around the site. I should have gotten some water and left, but for some reason, I couldn't bring myself to leave quite yet.

There was a change in the air, indicating a new presence. I headed toward the middle of the camp, curious. I remembered Bane told me that some prince of the fae was coming to camp. Maybe he would have answers that I needed.

When I approached, there was already a group of beings standing there, huddled together. I approached cautiously, my training taking over me. In the middle of the group, there was a tall, imposing man. He was dressed in all dark colors, his aura exuding confidence.

I was about twenty yards away, when he turned his head, eyes training on me. They were dark and piercing. I wasn't sure who this was, but I felt slightly shaken. I wasn't scared of him, just wary.

"This must be the Valkyrie." His voice was certain.

Bane gave him the confirmation he was apparently looking for.

The man stepped forward and the crowd parted. He walked in my direction, staring at me with a look that would wither a weaker being. Once he was boot to boot with me, he spoke.

"I am Crispin. The prince of the Seelie and Unseelie courts. Future king of the Unseelie court." He gave me a slight bow.

So, this was the prince. Not what I had expected. I supposed that I would see if he had what it took to be a leader.

Chapter 13

I studied the man standing in front of me. I wasn't sure what it was about him, but I suspected that he was more than just one type of creature. He had a power emanating from him, which sent chills up my arms. It was close to the same feeling I got being around the gods, but not as intense.

"I'm Kara."

"Join us and talk strategy. A Valkyrie is a very handy thing to have when in a battle." He turned and walked back to the group.

I followed, surprised that he was so willing to allow me into his plans. He knew nothing of me or what my actual intentions were, which I had every intention of pointing out to him. A leader shouldn't be as fool hardy as this. I also was going to point out that he should never turn his back to an unknown being. Doing so ran the risk of getting a sword, arrow, or other weapon in it.

I wouldn't mention it in front of his people, however. There was no reason to question his authority with followers in earshot. I would pull him to the side later.

"I'm glad you hadn't left yet. I heard so much about you from Bane and wanted to see the mythical Valkyrie in person. It was hard to believe that one was actually gracing us with her presence. My grandmother assured me that you were real, then Christine verified it." He didn't turn in my direction to speak with me.

His immediate trust made sense though. The oracle had probably told him what she had seen when she touched me. I hadn't thought about the gifts an oracle had. She would have been able to see everything, so she would know about Thor. Hopefully my marriage wouldn't ruin my credibility.

We spent the next several hours going over the plans and the best way to approach the demonic camp. I wanted to see them succeed so I gave them everything I could think of to help. The army they were going up against reminded me of the army of the dead that Loki had brought to Asgard.

When the group dispersed to prepare, I was left alone with Crispin. "Thank you for including me. I appreciate that you believe in my expertise."

He glanced at me as he was rolling up a map. "Your kind is a force to be reckoned with. This is the turn we need to change the tide. I believe that we will have a better chance now. So, do you want to tell me why you are really on Earth."

"Oh, you mean Midgard? It's a long story." I wanted to evade the topic of home.

"I have some time."

"Asgard is no more."

His gaze sharpened. It felt like his eyes were burning through me. "What do you mean?"

"Have you heard of Ragnarök?"

He gave me a nod, a frown forming on his face.

"It happened. They came, they destroyed, we fled. Now we are left to pick up the pieces and try to rebuild our lives. Families are broken, loved ones gone. We are scattered, scared, and lost in a land that only few have traveled to. It is a lot to take in and adjust to."

"Sounds familiar. My family fled from our original home when I was born. Mother and Father had to adjust to a new world, lifestyle. They are thriving now though."

"Good to know."

"So, what are you doing now? What are your plans?"

I stepped from side to side. "Honestly, I am looking for answers. I am trying to locate where Loki went. I'm not convinced he perished in Asgard. Then I have to look for my family. I don't know if they survived."

"Your family? I thought Valkyries didn't have families. They were just warriors."

"My situation is—" I hesitated. "a bit unusual. I'm sure your oracle has filled you in on it already."

"I want to hear it from you. I've found that stories mean more when they come from the person that they happened to. It gives the listener a better perspective of what happened. Also, it seems bizarre to me."

"Before we fled, I was wed to Thor, God of Thunder. We were married by Odin just hours before his death. Before we even had the chance to spend the night together as husband and wife, the battle ensued, and Thor was injured. He went through the Rainbow Bridge and Bi-Frost with one of my sister Valkyries. I have no idea if he is even alive still."

"That is quite a story. I apologize you have to deal with this. What I can do for you is, I can keep an eye out for your husband and pass along the word of your well-being when I come across him. I travel a lot, and rather swiftly, so I may run into him soon."

"Thank you, Majesty."

"Thank you for your help."

Without another word, I turned and walked away without looking back. I was wasting time here when I needed to be looking for Mist and Loki. I needed to find my husband. Heading into the woods, I hoped they would win the battle and push the demons back.

***

I didn't come across any other civilization in three days of walking. It was just trees and animals. The journey was peaceful; however, I was alone with my thoughts. That was what was scary about it. My mind still wandered to Mist and why she would betray us like she did.

The trees ended suddenly, and I was left walking through an open field. I felt vulnerable and exposed out there. There was a tingling at the base of my neck that told me I was being watched.

I felt a whoosh of air near my head, so I dropped to the ground in an effort to be partially concealed by the enemy. I strained my eyes, trying to catch a glimpse of my attacker. I couldn't see anyone. They must have been hiding in a bush or something.

I heard a rustle to my left. I reached for my sword but was surprised by an attack from the right. My attacker pounced on me, slamming my head into the unforgiving ground. Lights flashed in my eyes and my head started ringing.

Long, slimy fingers wrapped around my upper arm, flipping me onto my back. The wind was knocked out of me as I stared up at the ugliest creature I had ever seen. It was a greenish shade of black. The skin, well, what I thought was skin, was drooping off its face like a candle that had melted from the heat of the flame.

It smiled at me, its teeth yellowed and razor sharp. There was spittle and drool running from the side of its mouth. The smell emanating from it was making me want to vomit. I had never seen anything so vile in my life. It was worse than the army of the dead.

"Hades will enjoy this one. If not, then one of the guards will. Let's take her back to Hourglass City." His voice was raspy and slurred.

The thought of being taken to someone named Hades, and used for anything, freaked me out. I bucked and struggled to get away from him, but he just gripped me tighter. I noticed that my struggles were exciting him. This was a nightmare.

"Release me at once." I stopped fighting and laid there like a statue. My voice, surprisingly enough, was steady and calm.

"This one's funny. She thinks she can boss me around like I'm her puppet." He snickered, spittle flying all over my face.

When he stood and jerked me to my feet, my hand slid across my dagger. I grabbed it and pulled it from the sheath in one smooth movement. Swinging my arm, I slashed his throat with the edge of my blade. Black ooze squirted from the wound, spraying me in my face and eyes. I closed them quickly to try to keep them fluid free.

Before I had the chance to open my eyes again, the other creature had a grip on me. He wrapped one arm around my arms and chest, the other around my neck. Lifting me off the ground, he squeezed my neck, cutting off my air supply.

My vision began to tunnel and darken around the edges. I had been choked out enough during training to know I was about to lose consciousness. I hoped that this wasn't the end of my life. I had too much to do still.

***

When I opened my eyes again, I was in a cell that had a dirt floor and big metal door. I struggled to my feet, still feeling woozy from the blow to the head. Looking around, I tried to figure out where I was. There was no light except for a lantern sitting on the floor near me.

Picking up the lantern, I roamed around the cell, trying to get a feel for where I was. It was like nothing I had seen before. Granted I had never been arrested before, but the dungeon at Asgard was nothing like this.

There was a black puddle in one corner of the cell. Cautiously, I approached it, but not close enough to touch. Moving the lamp closer, I could see it wasn't black, but dark red. Then the smell hit me like a ton of bricks. It smelled like death. I was staring at someone's blood on the floor, soaking into the dirt.

My stomach threatened to revolt, but I fought it. There was no way in Helheim that I was going to give anyone the satisfaction of seeing any weakness. I had seen gods lying dead on the cold ground. Blood wasn't going to get to me.

Pacing the cell was supposed to burn some of my nervous energy. Instead, it was making me even more furious. Who in Helheim did they think they were to lock me into some hole like this! I was a Valkyrie, servant to the gods. I was protected. I was the wife of a god. I deserved respect.

Walking up to the door, I pounded on it with my fist. The noise echoed through the cell, and I was sure down the hall. "I beg pardon! I demand to speak with whomever is in charge."

I waited, listening to see if anyone would come to my door. When I didn't hear footsteps, I pounded on the door again. "When I said I wanted to speak with someone, I meant *now*!"

"Shut the fuck up, bitch." a voice from down the hallway barked at me. To my surprise, there was actual bark in the voice.

"I will not. I want to see your leader immediately."

"You ain't gonna like it, bitch." He chuckled, ending with a yip. "Or maybe you will."

The innuendo was so clear in that last statement, I didn't have to guess what he meant by it. He was being crude. If I weren't locked in the cell, I would have beat the living shit out of him. The disrespect was something that I wasn't used to. I wanted to slit his throat.

"Why don't you get him and let me find out for myself?" I tried to sound nonchalant but wasn't sure if I pulled it off. I wasn't used to this kind of situation and wasn't sure if I was handling it correctly.

There was a chuckle from the other side, then footsteps receding and echoing away. I waited, nervous energy building. I had the need to hit something. I shook my hands and rolled my neck, trying to loosen up in case I got the chance to fight.

Footsteps sounded through the cell, indicating that someone was approaching. They stopped right outside my cell. I almost wanted to hold my breath while I waited for the new visitor to speak.

"I'm going to open this door and enter. If you try anything stupid, you will regret it immensely." The voice was soft yet commanding and carried through the thick door. "Do you agree to my terms?"

"Why do you think I'd do something stupid?" I was genuinely curious to know his assessment of me. He wasn't completely wrong. I did make some rash decisions.

He laughed. It was a melodious sound that sent shivers of anticipation down my spine. "I am well aware of your actions since my people came across

107

you. I'll admit you are a feisty thing and I enjoy that. Do you agree?

"Yes."

The door began to open silently on well-oiled hinges. A man stood on the other side of the door. Stepping into the cell, his power washed over me. This man was extremely powerful. It had a feel to it that could rival Thor's. He was tall and lean.

His eyes were dark and mysterious. I couldn't help but wonder about him. Who was this strange man?

He approached me and studied me like you do when you come across a wild animal and aren't sure if it's going to attack you or not. His features went from neutral to pinched in a heartbeat.

"You wished to speak to me?" It was posed as a question, but it was actually a demand for an answer.

"I demand to be released at once." I lifted my chin, holding my head a little higher.

"Why should I release you, Valkyrie?"

I was taken aback by the fact that he knew what I was. I didn't think anyone in this world knew, being they hadn't come across us before. We stayed in Asgard the majority of the time.

"I was brought here by mistake. Release me and you will not have to face extreme consequences. "

"Why would anyone care that a Valkyrie, especially one as weak as you, disappeared?" He leaned closer and sniffed my hair. "You definitely weren't brought here by mistake."

I was revolted by the thought. They had meant for me to be used like a kept woman. "You are vile."

He smiled at me. It was disarming and charming at the same time. There was also a coldness to it that made the hair on the back of my neck stand on end. I took an involuntary step away from him before I realized I had done it.

"Now is that any way to talk to your host?"

"Who are you?"

"How rude of me. My name is Hades, and you are in my home. We are in Hourglass City, formerly known as the Underworld." He gave me a slight bow.

So, I was in Midgard's equivalent of Helheim. I wasn't completely surprised.

Chapter 14

I was in the underworld, or Hourglass City, as Hades called it. I wasn't sure why he would call it that, but it was a moot thought. I stared at him as he smiled at me. He didn't flinch or move, almost reminding me of a statue.

"Why did you want to see me?" he asked quietly. The smile faded and his eyes darkened.

"Release me."

"Why would I do that?"

"Because I demand it. I am a Valkyrie, and I will be respected."

"Valkyries are nothing here. They are just fairytales and stories that the humans used to tell their offspring."

"I am not just a story."

He sighed. "This is getting redundant."

"I agree. Now release me."

He backed away from me, toward the door. "I don't think so."

The door slammed with a resounding thud. I stood there, staring at the door, dumbfounded. It didn't make sense that he was going to leave me here. I was being held prisoner. I walked to the wall, punching it as hard as I could.

My hand made a crunch sound and pain shot up my arm. I was certain that I had just broken my hand on the wall. I pressed my back against the cool stone as the tears built up behind my eyes. Blinking them back didn't help, so I finally let them escape and roll down my cheeks.

In my moment of weakness, I slid down the wall until I was sitting, and wrapped my arms around my knees. I cried until I couldn't cry any longer. When the tears were done, I lifted my head and dried my eyes with the side of my hand.

The next step was to start planning. I had to find a way to escape. I couldn't stay here. I had to get out and find Mist. I needed to know that Thor was okay. It was killing me not knowing. I racked my brain, but nothing came to mind. I was going to have to figure this out.

I quickly lost track of time as I sat in the cell. I was barely fed, and water was minimal. I had to resort to conserving water and squirreling it away. It felt like I had been in there for an eternity, where time stood still.

The only indication that time was passing was the coming and going of the guards. No one spoke to me. The sound of silence was beginning to grate on my nerves. If I didn't get away soon, I was sure I would go stark raving mad.

The cell door opened slowly, causing my head to jerk up in surprise. My meal, if you could call the stale disgusting crumbs that, had just been delivered a little while ago. Two burly guards with heads of dogs stood there staring at me.

"Come," one hissed at me. His voice reminded me of a snake.

A bad feeling washed over me as I stared at the two brutes. I knew going with them was a horrible idea. It was probably my only chance to escape, but at what cost?

"N-n," I cleared my throat to try again. "No, thank you."

My voice had cracked and sounded rusty from lack of use. It actually hurt to speak.

The guards came closer, each one grabbing an arm, pulling me to my feet. Out of training and instinct, I tried to fight myself free, to no avail. I was simply too weak from malnourishment. Their grips tightened to the point I was sure I would bruise.

"It's not a choic-c-c-c-c-e," the guard that spoke before said.

They dragged me from the cell, down a long hallway. We went through a door where there was a chair sitting in the middle of the room. The chair had straps attached to it, for holding its occupant down. There was this weird looking machine over the right arm.

They pushed me into the chair, one holding me while the other strapped me in. Once I was secure, they stepped back and disappeared into the shadows. I looked around, trying to see if there was a way for me to escape, but I wasn't sitting by myself for long.

A red-skinned demon approached the chair and loomed over me. He had ritualistic type tattoos covering his body. They appeared to be slightly raised off his skin. I bet if I ran my hand over it, I would have been able to feel the design.

One of the tattoos on his chest caught my eye. It was a giant clock. What caught my attention was that the pendulum gently swayed back and forth. The longer I stared at the clock, I swore I saw the minute hand move.

He moved closer to me, grabbing a handle on the machine next to the chair. Pulling it down, he pressed it against my skin. The burning was instantaneous, I wanted to scream and cry, but my pride wouldn't let me. I bit my lip to keep the sounds in.

When he lifted it from my arm, there was a burn mark in the shape of an hourglass. It was red and angry. Little blisters were bubbling up along the lines of the brand. The sound the demon made had me looking up at him with watery eyes.

He was frowning at the mark like he was confused. He shoved it back down onto my forearm, making me flinch and inhale sharply. It felt like a thousand burning needles piercing my skin all at once. When he lifted it, the mark didn't look much different, just redder.

"What the bloody hell?" he asked. I was sure he wasn't asking me though.

The door burst open as he was lowering the contraption down on my arm for the third time. He stopped mid-movement, glaring at the door.

I turned my head toward the door to see a tall shadowy figure standing there. The light from the torches behind him were causing the shadows to fall over him so his face was concealed. The only movement in the room was the light flickering.

He stepped into the room, tension thickening with each long step of his. When he made it to the chair, his face was now in the light. He had similar features to Hades, just as dark and brooding.

"What is going on here?" His voice held an air of authority. He spoke softly, but I didn't need to strain to hear him.

"I have orders to mark her, my prince." The demon seemed nervous suddenly. He was shifting on his feet and his eyes darted around, not settling on one thing.

"Whose orders?" The man crossed his arms and rocked back on his heels. The gesture was an intimidating one.

"Your father gave the command. I am just a lowly servant."

He laughed then. "My father isn't stupid enough to try to end a Valkyrie with the hourglass trick. He would have come up with something more creative. The tattoo doesn't work on them like it does others. Now release her and I will deal with her from here."

The threat was clear, but I wasn't sure whom it was aimed at. I hoped it wasn't me. I was also confused by his words. I didn't know what an hourglass trick was.

My attention was brought back to the demon when the warmth of his hand made my arm scream in pain. I jerked my head his way. He was unstrapping my arm. As soon as both were free, I swung with an open palm, smashing the heel of my hand into his enormous nose.

Boiling hot blood shot out of it, spraying on me, but I didn't care. It felt marvelous to release some of the energy I had been holding back. My leg shot up, my shin connecting to his groin. He doubled over and fell to his knees.

When he regained his feet, he growled at me. "Bitch, you're dead."

"Do *not* touch her!" the man shouted as his arms dropped from across his chest. His hands balled into fists and he started to change color. His skin started blackening and red lines appeared, marring the smooth black shade. His eyes turned completely black, flames dancing in them.

The red demon dropped to his knees, bowing and groveling at his feet. "I beg forgiveness, my prince."

"Leave us." His voice boomed and echoed through the room almost like thunder. It reminded me a little of when Thor was angry. The demon vanished in a puff of smoke.

When we were alone, the man, the prince, walked over and held his hand out to me. I hesitated. I wasn't sure what to do. I watched as his skin went back to the original color.

"Let me help you."

My hand trembled slightly as I put it in his. His long fingers curled around mine, helping me out of the chair. His grip was gentle yet firm. Once I was on my feet, he wrapped an arm around my waist and led me out the door.

We didn't speak as we walked. He led me at a brisk pace. Passing through hallways, he didn't take time to pause at intersections or hesitate when making turns. It was obvious he knew where he was going, while it felt like a maze to me.

Once we were outside, I expected grass, sunshine, fresh air. What we had was darkness, heat, rocks, fire. It was terrifying. I looked around, taking it all in. I was having trouble processing everything. Confusion washed over me. I had no idea what was going on.

"Keep walking, the alarm will go off at any minute." the man spoke quietly. I glanced his way but lost my footing and almost fell. He righted me but didn't stop. "Come on, we are almost there. Just a little further."

We slipped into an alley before we finally came to a halt. My breathing was heavy. I hadn't realized how out of shape and sick I had been until we stopped.

"Are you alright?"

I nodded. Lifting my head, I made eye contact with him. "Why are you helping me? Who are you?"

"I'm Lucian. I'm helping you because there was no reason for you to be locked away. You are innocent of any wrongdoing and I won't let my father make you into one of his playthings."

I frowned.

"He likes to break the will of strong ones and then use them as puppets. I couldn't let him do that to you. His sick games annoy me." He ran a hand through his hair. "Besides, I believe that my good mate, Crispin, has been looking for you for a while."

"Crispin?" The fae flashed through my head.

"Aye. He heard rumors of a Valkyrie being taken and had a feeling it was you. Said you helped him with something, so he owed you." He glanced around the alley. "He should be here any moment."

"Thank you, Lucian." I swallowed then spoke again. "I appreciate all you have done for me."

"You're welcome. Now you need to know something about Hourglass City and the Underworld."

"What?"

"Time passes differently here. Slower. It's part of the whole Hell and punishment thing. I'm not exactly sure how long you've been here, but I believe you have been here around one hundred Earth years."

I felt the color drain from my face. "One hundred years?"

"Yes. Give or take. Like I said, I wasn't made known of your imprisonment until yesterday. I was at the academy, then on the battlefield."

The air pressure changed, and the next thing I knew, Crispin was standing there. It didn't feel like it had been more than a week since I had seen him, but there were some slight changes in him. He appeared more muscular, less innocent.

"Kara, I am glad to see you. When I heard the demons got you, I started tracking you. I'm sorry it took so long to find you." Crispin said with a slight bow.

"All is well. I was planning my escape."

Crispin smiled. "I'm sure you were right near escaping. Now come. We need to get out of here.

Lucian will do his best to delay the notice of your disappearance."

I took a couple of unsteady steps toward Crispin. He slipped an arm around my waist, holding me up.

"Thank you, brother," Crispin nodded at Lucian.

"You are quite welcome. Now get out of here. Get her somewhere my father wouldn't dare to chase her."

Crispin's arms wrapped around me and, next thing I knew, we were standing outside a giant glass dome. Inside the dome was a city which looked to be built from gold, pearls, and clouds. I looked back at Crispin with confusion on my face.

"Hades won't follow you here. I can't go in because I don't get along the best with the gods. This is New Olympus." He looked toward the city. "When you get in there, look for a woman named Crimson. She will get you where you need to go."

I nodded; words were not needed. I turned toward the dome and walked carefully across the bridge into it. Halfway across, my head began to spin, and my knees buckled. As everything went dark, I heard Crispin swear.

Chapter 15

Opening my eyes, my head spun. I struggled to sit up, but gentle hands pushed me back down onto the mattress. I finally focused on the person hovering over me. She had hair the color of fresh blood. Her eyes seemed to glow from an inner light.

"You need to rest. You are parched and starved. There is a spot on your arm that looks to be infected." Her voice was gentle and soothing. "Here's some water. Drink slowly. I don't want you getting ill and vomiting the water back up from drinking too quickly."

She helped me lift my head a little and brought the cup to my mouth. The cold water was glorious. I gulped until the cup was empty. She lowered my head back down.

"What happened?" I asked slowly. My head pounded at the sound of my own voice.

"From what Prince Crispin told me, you were held prisoner by Hades, the rat bastard. When you were brought here, you passed out on the way into the city." She brushed my hair back, then pressed the back of her hand to my forehead. "You have a fever, so you need to rest more. The fever should break soon."

"I have to go," I struggled to sit up again. Her hand came down onto my shoulder and pushed me back.

"You must rest. You were locked up for a long time. It will take a while to recover from that."

I stopped resisting when my head began to spin, and laid back down, closing my eyes. The room tilted to the left, then spun in a circle a few times until it finally settled down. As my mind began to drift, before sleep overcame me, I had to know. "Are you Crimson?"

"Yes, now sleep."

"Have you heard how Thor, God of Thunder, is doing?"

"He's—" She paused for a moment. "He's alive."

The way she answered wasn't a comfort to me. I wanted to ask more, but exhaustion washed over me. All thoughts were lost as I fell into a deep sleep.

When I woke up again, there was sunlight streaming into the room. I sat up and shook my head a little to clear the fuzzies that seemed to have gathered there. I blinked the sleep away and stood up.

Standing felt funny for a moment. I looked around the room. The woman, Crimson, sat at the table, the sunlight shining off her hair. I slowly approached the table.

When I made it to the table, Crimson spoke without looking up. "Sit, I'll get you breakfast. You need to regain your strength."

I sat at the table. It reminded me of the table at Valhalla, but on a much smaller scale. It was scarred and worn. I couldn't help but smile as I ran my fingers over the indentations. I was certain there were some great memories that went along with each mark.

A plate was set in front of me, filled with bacon and eggs. My stomach growled and cramped from the smell. I hadn't realized how ravenous I was until that moment. The aroma of the food made my mouth water. The plate was empty before I realized what happened.

A piece of toast was handed to me, and I ate it much slower than I had the rest of the food.

I realized that Crimson was watching me. I set the toast down on the plate and took a sip of the water that was sitting there.

"Thank you. I appreciate your hospitality. Can you give me an update of what I missed while I was away?" I couldn't bring myself to use the word imprisoned. It was too difficult to speak about.

"Well, we figure you were there for close to one hundred years. I know it didn't seem like that long, but time is a fickle thing." She glanced out the window. "The war ended, but the humans are few and far between now. The ones that did survive have gone into hiding. The demons were pushed back, but the threat still looms."

"What about Thor? And the other Valkyries?" I wasn't ready to deal with the fact that I had been locked up for that long. I just wanted to believe that I had only been there a few days.

"I'm not sure how much I should actually tell you. It's been a rough century."

"I want to know the truth, all of it."

She nodded, then stood up. She paced the small room, suddenly acting nervous. It didn't bode well for me. I watched her pace, causing my nerves to start to flare up.

"Well," she stopped and looked at me for several heartbeats. "Thor has made his home in Thunder Valley. He has been in quite the mood since he woke up. They say that he has destroyed much in his misery."

"What happened to him?" My heart was racing with the thought that something horrible was wrong with him.

"He's heartbroken. Apparently, his wife died when Asgard was attacked, and he's been mourning her for the last hundred years. I've only heard stories, but from what I've heard, he's gone a little mad."

I shook my head furiously. "No. His wife isn't dead."

"She is. She didn't make it."

"I'm his wife. He's been misinformed. Crispin was supposed to tell him I was alive and well."

She nodded. "I have no doubt he tried to give him the word. By the time Crispin was able to talk to him, however, he had already been told of your death and believed that Crispin was late delivering the word, or simply didn't believe him."

I almost dreaded asking the next question. "What about the Valkyries?"

"You aren't going to like this."

"Like I've liked anything else you have told me so far." I stood and approached her. I took her hands and looked into her eyes. "Crimson, I need to know. They are my sisters."

She sighed heavily before speaking. "The majority of them were brought into New Olympus as slaves. They work for the Greek gods."

"And the rest?"

"Dead or in hiding. Some were made examples of. Zeus didn't like that they wouldn't just immediately bow down to him and the Greeks."

I nodded. Sounded like I had a lot of work to do. First things first, I needed to speak with this Zeus. "Take me to him."

"Kara, that's not a good idea. He may enslave you as well."

"I dealt with Hades, the army of the dead, Loki, betrayal, Fenrir, and many other nightmares you can only imagine. I think Zeus will be easy."

"If you insist, but I won't let you go by yourself. I'm going with you."

"Thank you."

Crimson packed a quick satchel to take with us before we headed out. I watched her with interest. She placed weapons that were unfamiliar to me in it. I didn't think she would be able to get them past the guards, but it was worth a shot at any rate.

We headed out, walking the streets of New Olympus. I couldn't help but look around. There were so many things to look at. Everything seemed to shine and shimmer, reminding me of diamonds.

"Why is there a protective layer around this city?" Curiosity was eating at me.

Crimson shrugged with one shoulder. "To keep those they want out, out, I guess. The Greeks are a finicky bunch. They are snobs and only like certain beings. They despise fae and the majority of the supernatural creatures. They believe the supernaturals are beneath them. They believe everything is beneath them."

I had a feeling this wasn't going to go over well, but I was going to do it anyway. I had never backed down from a fight. I wasn't going to start now.

As we approached the palace, my stomach did a small flip. The palace reminded me a lot of the palace at Asgard. Instead of gold, it was made from glass and diamond. In my opinion, it was too flashy and overdone. It was not created tastefully.

The way it was designed made me think they just wanted attention from the building. There didn't appear to be any efficiency to the building. Walking up the marble steps, I frowned to myself. There was no traction and in an emergency, people trying to evacuate would have trouble staying on their feet.

The doors opened on their own. I glanced at Crimson before stepping across the threshold. The doors closed behind us as well. We walked through the hall, not seeing a single being on the way. It seemed odd that there was no one there. It was midday and people should have been milling about.

We approached the doors to the grand hall. I stopped and stared at the intricate carvings in the wood of the door. They were a beautiful mahogany. I was surprised to see something not made out of marble, or gold, or diamond.

Pushing the door open, I strode into the room. Once in the room, I looked around and locked eyes with a servant. It took several heartbeats to recognize her. Sanngrid. If it weren't for the fire in her eyes, I wouldn't have recognized her at all. She had a collar around her neck.

Sanngrid's eyes widened as we stared at each other. She looked as if she had seen a ghost. I wanted to hug her, reassure her that I was going to get her out of there. If I had my way, I would take her out of the building with me when I left.

I approached the row of gods sitting on the dais. I went straight toward the one sitting on the throne in the center. His throne was placed higher up, a not-so-subtle sign of his superiority and station. I dropped on one knee and lowered my head in a gesture of respect.

"I am Kara," I raised my head so I could look at the god in question.

"What do you wish to see me about? It is unbecoming of you to show up to demand an audience without notice. You look like nothing but a pathetic weak woman." Zeus looked down at me condescendingly.

I rose then. If he was going to be rude and blunt, I was going to be the same. Technically, I was a higher station than most that requested an audience.

"We have a problem."

Leaning forward, his eyes narrowed at me. "I do not see a problem. What problem do you think we have?"

"First off, you have been in complete disregard of my station, which given my circumstances, I understand. Secondly, you have taken my people and turned them into slaves."

"What people do you speak of?"

"The Valkyries."

One eyebrow slowly raised. "Valkyries?"

"Did I forget to mention that I am Kara, wife of Thor, God of Thunder? I am one of the surviving Valkyries of Ragnarök. I demand that my people be freed."

"Kara, wife of Thor, I find it amusing that you claim to be the wife of the God of Thunder, not that I acknowledge the Norse gods, yet he has made it clear his wife is dead."

I took a deep breath, trying to remain calm. My eyes shot to Hades, sitting on the end of the line. His throne was black with skulls hanging off it and what appeared to be a decapitated head. The eyes were staring at me. "That is a misunderstanding, one that we can thank the caring, considerate Hades for."

"Care to explain?"

"No. Hades can fill in the blanks for you if you must know. I don't have time to discuss it. I have a list of things to do, since I am finally free to do as I wished when I first arrived at Midgard." I redirected my gaze at the formidable Zeus. "My first order of business is to demand the freedom of my Valkyries."

"Why would I release my servants?"

I took a step closer to him. "They are not your servants. They are my people. I will not leave without them. If there is some reason I do walk out of here alone today, I will not be coming back alone. There will be bloodshed like you've never seen before. You think the fight against the demons was messy, try a scorned Valkyrie."

"What will a Valkyrie do to a god?"

"We have been known as the killers of gods. We spent our lifetimes training for the big fight, to protect what is ours. I will do whatever I can do to get my people back."

He leaned back in his chair and stroked his long beard with his hand. "Now, I am not an unreasonable god. I will show you that I can be fair. However, I will not release all of my servants, just one."

"I will take Sanngrid."

"I will choose whom to free." He raised a hand and made a gesture.

Two guards drug in a slave. Her long hair was listless and stringy. They held her by the arms, her knees dragging on the ground. There was a trail of blood behind her, assumingly coming from her knees. When they got to the base of the dais, they dropped her on the ground. One gave her a swift kick to the ribs.

She grunted and rolled to her side. It took all I had not to react when I saw her face. Brynhild. She was just skin and bones. Her cheeks were hollowed out and her eyes sunk in from malnourishment. Her features were almost indistinguishable behind the bruising and swelling. She looked like she had been made over more than once.

I knelt beside her, gently brushing her hair back from her face. Her head jerked away from me out of reflex.

Leaning over her, I whispered in her ear, "I am taking you somewhere safe. I am going to take care of you. You will be fine, sister."

Slowly, I stood back up. My breathing had quickened as anger raced through me. I imagined slitting their throats and burning the new, shiny city around them. Glancing at Crimson, she raced over to Brynhild, practically lifting her.

I turned, starting to walk away but stopped and faced Sanngrid. "Stand. We are leaving."

She looked at me, then looked at the man holding the leash attached to the collar. I could feel her indecision emanating from her. The man jerked on the leash. She crouched closer to the ground.

I walked up to them, not thinking about what I was doing. My fist shot out and made contact with his nose. I pulled a dagger from my boot while I was shoving him toward the wall. I pressed the dagger against his Adam's apple.

"Sanngrid, go to Crimson and Brynhild. You are leaving with us now." I didn't take my eyes off the man. "You utter a word, and I will slit your throat. You will be dead before you have a chance to blink."

Once I felt like she had gotten far enough away, I released the man and stepped back. I turned and walked to my little group, helping Sanngrid to her feet and wrapping my arm around her waist. As we slowly made our way out of the room, I could feel eyes burning into the back of my head. I refused to give them the satisfaction of me looking back.

I made a silent vow that I was going to come back and kill all of them. Even if it killed me, I would see the Valkyries free.

CHAPTER 16

O nce leaving the palace, I decided staying in New Olympus would be a mistake. I didn't trust the Greeks. Those gods seemed shady. We made our way out into the woods. After hours of walking, I took pity on Brynhild and Sanngrid. They had been doing their best to keep moving and not fall behind, but exhaustion and fatigue were taking over.

I let them rest while Crimson and I made camp. The fire was built quickly and once everything was set, I went hunting. We all needed to keep up our strength for the journey ahead. I managed to get a couple of small animals and brought them back to camp.

During our meal, I kept my eyes on Brynhild. She had been thoroughly abused. Her body was battered and beaten. Her ribs were prominent from not being fed. I feared that she would get a fever or be overcome by her illness.

"Get some rest. We must start traveling again when the sun rises. Crimson, do you know the way to Thunder Valley?" I chewed slowly, while waiting on her answer

She nodded. "Aye. It's a long journey from here. Too long on foot. However, we may be able to get assistance. I will go see if I can get any of my contacts to help."

"You do that. We need to get to Thor and back to free the Valkyries. I will keep watch tonight."

Crimson slipped into the shadows and disappeared. After the other two finished eating and fell asleep, I had plenty of time to do some thinking. I was anxious to see Thor again. I hoped that he still loved me. I still couldn't wrap my mind around the fact that I had been locked away for a hundred years. That was a long time, even for an immortal.

Closing my eyes, I imagined what it would be like to see Thor again. Doubts began creeping in. I didn't know if he would believe I was really alive, or if he really had gone crazy. Maybe he didn't want to see me. If he had fallen in love with someone else, it would kill me. Literally. I would have nothing else to live for.

"You're thinking too loud, little one." Brynhild spoke quietly. If the woods hadn't been silent, I wouldn't have heard her.

I turned my head and looked in her direction. She was sitting up, but I doubted she could see anything with her eyes swollen as they were. "What?"

"You're thinking too loud. I could have snuck up and slit your throat and you would have never seen it coming."

I chuckled. "I doubt you can do any sneaking in the condition that you are in, but I see your point."

"You were thinking about Thor, weren't you?"

"Aye."

"I stayed with him until he was healed. He was furious when he found out you stayed behind in Asgard. I told him what you did. He wanted you by his side. If you are worried he's moved on or something silly like that, don't. His heart is broken.

When I last saw him, he was still determined to find you."

"You're just trying to make me feel better."

She chuckled then. "I don't like you that much, Kara. You have always been a pain in my ass."

"I know."

"Kara." I looked back at her. Her smile had disappeared, and she had a serious air to her. "Thank you. For not only saving me, but for saving Sanngrid as well. She probably wouldn't have survived much longer. Neither would I."

"No need to thank me. You would have done the same thing. Any of us would have. Brynhild," I paused and took a deep breath. I felt like a little girl scared of the shadows. "Do you know why Mist betrayed us?"

She sighed heavily. "I don't. I can only guess. Once everyone else is free, you should go ask her. She is living with Loki at Illusion Forest. She has been living as his queen."

"I plan on it." I smiled softly at her. "Now get some sleep and regain your strength. We're going to need it for the journey and battle ahead."

After she was back asleep, I sat and stared into the darkness until the sun began to rise. After putting out the fire and gathering fruits for breakfast, I made sure Sanngrid and Brynhild were awake. They got up and began to eat without a word passing between them.

As the sun rose higher in the sky, I started to wonder what happened to Crimson. I figured she would have returned by now. We wouldn't be able to wait much longer before we continued our journey. I didn't know where to head; I hoped that Brynhild did, since she had been to this Thunder Valley.

When the sun was firmly set in the morning sky, I decided it was time to get moving. The longer we sat here, the more likely attacks were going to be. I couldn't risk my injured people any more harm.

"We need to get moving," I studied both women for a moment. "Sanngrid, can you walk unassisted?"

She gave me a slight nod, but didn't speak. The more I thought about it, I realized that she hadn't uttered a peep this whole time.

"Is your voice alright?"

She shook her head no and patted her throat with two fingers.

I frowned. I wasn't sure what she was trying to convey but we needed to get her medical assistance as soon as possible. "Alright. Let's get moving. I'll help Brynhild. Sanngrid, do your best to walk on your own. We are going to move slowly, but it's best we go now."

Helping Brynhild to her feet, her legs gave. She would have hit the ground if I hadn't already had a grip on her. I cursed under my breath and helped her up again. She wrapped and arm around my shoulders for support and attempted to move of her own accord. We were able to take small painfully slow steps. I debated on whether carrying her was a better option than this. If we continued at this pace, we would never make it to Thunder Valley.

We had only gone a few feet when there was a rustling in the tree line. Reaching down, I grabbed the dagger in my boot and pulled it out quickly. I held it out in a defensive stance. I would fight anything that came through the trees if it meant protecting my people.

Crimson appeared in the clearing with a short ugly creature. He had pointed ears and looked like he was a thousand years old.

"Sorry it took so long. Octavious here wouldn't believe me about helping Valkyries and insisted on seeing for himself before agreeing to help us."

"What is he?" I asked, squinting at him.

"I, my dear Valkyrie, am a gnome. It is truly a pleasure to meet you."

I gave him a slight nod in greeting, grip tightening a little on Brynhild. She was dead weight and felt heavier every passing second. I wouldn't be able to hold her for any amount of time. I didn't want to be rude by hurrying him along, but at the same time, I was ready to be on our way.

"What do you have for us to travel on?"

"This," he waved his hand and a unicorn and centaur both walked up.

I stood in awe of the majestic greatness in front of me. I had never seen a unicorn or centaur before. The centaur approached and took Brynhild from me, holding her as if she weighed no more than a babe. He didn't speak, just nodded at me. I gave a slight nod back to him.

"Let us go. It is a long journey, and we need to make some distance before the sun sets." The centaur turned and began walking from the direction in which they came.

"Wait," I called out, stepping forward. "What shall I call you? I don't believe that centaur is an appropriate way to address one. I believe in the power of a name."

"I am Casos." He smiled as he said it.

"I am Kara," I couldn't help but smile back.

We started our journey. I couldn't help but to be amazed by the entourage that I had unintentionally collected. There was a woman, gnome, centaur, and the two other Valkyries. As nice as it was to have the company, I was worried that these unsuspecting creatures would end up getting hurt or killed since they were around me. This was my battle, not theirs.

We made camp as the sun was beginning to set. Casos held Brynhild until a makeshift bed was set up for her. He placed her on the bed gently and glided into the trees, disappearing. I watched him for a moment before I continued to make the fire.

There was a spark, and the kindling began to smoke. I leaned forward and gently blew on it, hoping that the puff of air would feed the beginning flames. Within moments, the flame grew and built until it was a sustainable fire.

I sat back on my haunches and watched the flames dance to life. It was always a gratifying feeling accomplishing making fire. It was something that helped sustain life. As I watched the flames, I thought about Thor. I wondered how he was and what he was doing right then.

My heart ached when thoughts of him came to mind. I mentally shook myself, trying to get him off my mind. I couldn't afford to allow myself to think about him or I would be completely useless. I needed to have patience and perseverance. I knew that eventually I would get to see him again, but I wouldn't be able to be with him until I accomplished my mission and freed the Valkyries.

"Kara?" The voice was soft and scratchy. I turned and looked into the troubled eyes of Sanngrid.

"Yes?"

"I want to apologize for never believing in you. You were always carefree and headstrong, I never believed that you would do what was needed and be a good Valkyrie. I was wrong. You are probably one of the strongest I have ever met. Thank you for saving me."

I took her hand and held it in both of mine. "You are very welcome, Sanngrid. I know what everyone believed. All is forgiven. I need you to gain your strength and be prepared to fight to free the others. Now eat and rest, sister."

She didn't move, just shifted her eyes toward the fire. We sat quietly watching the flames dance in the way only fire could.

CHAPTER 17

As we neared what they called Thunder Valley, the sky became angry. Clouds blocked the sun and sky, causing a tension and heaviness in the air. It was oppressive, but we pushed on. We were less than a day's journey away from the valley when the rains began.

The rain came down in sheets so heavy that we had to take shelter in a cave to try to be protected from it. I wanted to press on and get there so Brynhild and Sanngrid could get the treatment they so needed. I also knew how close I was to reuniting with my love.

I stared out into the rain while the others rested and attempted to sleep. I could hear Brynhild whimpering and moaning softly in her sleep. She wouldn't admit it to anyone, but the pain had to be excruciating. She still hadn't gained consciousness for more than a short period at a time, but she needed the healing sleep.

A hand rested on my shoulder. Looking up to see who it was, I found Crimson standing there, smiling down at me. She stepped even with me, then seated herself so we were touching shoulder to shoulder.

"You seem to have a lot on your mind, Kara. Care to share?" Her voice had a soothing cadence to it that helped settle my nerves.

"I don't know how Thor is going to receive me. He thinks I am dead. How am I supposed to tell him that it's not true? What is he going to think when he finds out I've been held captive for all this time? Will he think less of me?" I sighed and rolled my neck, listening to it pop.

"He will receive you well. He is your husband. A love doesn't go away because of circumstances. He will be angry as to why you were gone but will be relieved to have his wife back. There is no way he will think less of you. If anything, he will admire your strength for lasting as long as you did under Hades's care. I promise you, reuniting with him will go well."

"I also fear that reuniting with him won't be as easy as we hope. I can't explain why, but I have a feeling that I will not be making it to Thunder Valley now."

"Don't say that. You know you are going to make it. As soon as the rain lets up, we will finish our journey and go to the valley. Once there, we can get the troops and go back to free the Valkyries."

I studied Crimson's profile. She wasn't an old woman, yet she wasn't young either. I wasn't sure how old she was, but she had fine lines around her eyes. Her hair reminded me of blood. I hadn't thought much about why she was so invested in this journey with me or why. She wasn't a Valkyrie. As far as I knew, she wasn't a supernatural of any kind. She was simply a Midgardian. Midgardians were fragile things.

"Why are you helping me?"

She turned to face me then. Her gaze pierced into mine. "It is my destiny to help you."

"What are you?"

A small, secretive smile formed on her face. "That is my cross to bear for the moment. All will be revealed in time. Just know that I am on your side."

"And I thank you for that."

The silence that filled the cave was a peaceful one, both of us lost in our own thoughts. I couldn't shake the feeling of impending doom that was creeping up on me. It was the same feeling I had had when Ragnarök was beginning.

Thunder rolled and rumbled, causing the ground to shake. The hair on the back of my neck stood up as the rumbling got louder.

"Crimson, go with the others in the back of the cave. Don't make a sound. Keep Brynhild and Sanngrid quiet." I instructed as I rose to my feet.

She stood next to me, watching me. Concern was written all over her face. "Kara, what's wrong?"

"That isn't thunder. It's horses. We have company coming and it isn't going to be pleasant. I will hold them off. Once it's clear, go to Thor. Explain what has happened. He will know what to do."

She nodded, then hugged me. I returned the hug. Once she released me, I watched her run into the shadows of the cave. There were rushed whispers, but they stopped quickly. I studied the darkness for a moment before I turned, pulling my dagger from its sheath. It was then I wished that I had my sword or bow.

As I stepped into the rain, I glanced up, sending a prayer to whoever or whatever would listen. I hoped to see Thor again, even though I was doubtful it would happen. There was a part of me that hoped Thor heard my prayer and came to find me. I knew that wouldn't happen though, since he thought me dead.

The rain pelted me. I was drenched in seconds. I couldn't see more than a foot in front of me. I listened, trying to figure out where the horses were coming from and how far away so I could lead them away from the cave. I couldn't chance them getting too close to the others.

It sounded like they were coming from the east, so I ran south. As I ran, the rain hit me like small knives, stabbing me in the face. It was ice cold, chilling me to the bone. I dodged tree stumps and fallen logs, making as much noise as possible to steer them toward me.

I still wasn't sure who they were, but I wasn't taking any chances. My top priority was protecting everyone. I jumped over a trunk, my boot catching on a branch that I hadn't seen or expected. I landed face first in a mud puddle, my dagger shooting out of my hand into the underbrush.

Struggling, I lifted myself out of the mud, trying to wipe it out of my eyes. I spat a chunk of mud out of my mouth. There was also a metallic taste to it. Blood. I must have bitten the inside of my cheek on the landing. Untangling my foot, I managed to get to my feet as the sound of hooves neared and slowed.

I glanced around for my dagger, but I couldn't find it. I mentally cursed myself for not having a better grip on my weapon or extra weapons on my person. Or had extra weapons, period. This was going to get messy.

I was surrounded and unarmed. I was going to have to fight my way out of it with my bare hands. It wasn't going to be pretty, and I knew that I was going to end up getting hurt. My goal was to at least limp out of the fight in one piece.

I made a step forward when all the men surrounding me drew their weapons. I took a deep breath, letting it out slowly as I prepared myself for battle.

The first attack came quick, and I was easily able to fend it off. I disarmed him, taking control of his sword. It felt good having a weapon in my hand. It was like an extension to my arm.

The rest of the soldiers descended on me. I swung the sword with all my might. The blade bit into its mark, causing blood to spray in an arc. The next soldier, I was able to impale through the chest.

As soon as I thought I stood a chance at winning, more soldiers showed up. I lost a moment of concentration when I heard a scream in the distance. It was the distraction they needed to take me down.

One moment, I was on my feet and in the next, I was on the ground, dagger at my throat, swords surrounding me, all pointed at me. I could feel the cold steel of a blade digging into my upper thigh. If they pushed down, I'd bleed out in moments.

"Surrender yourself and I'll let you live." A voice boomed through the woods over the rain and thunder.

Turning in the direction the voice came from, I tried to pinpoint who was speaking. I couldn't tell. All the soldiers wore hoods or some sort of masks. They were all motionless. If I hadn't just fought them, I would think they were statues. It was eerie how still they were.

I considered my options. If I surrendered, I would live to die another day at this stranger's hands. If I fought to the death, I'd be dead. I wasn't sure which choice would be the better one. The blade that was pressing against my thigh bit into me a little harder. I felt the small pop as it broke the skin. The warm blood slid down the inside of my thigh. It was pretty clear that my options were limited. I was going to have to yield and come up with a new plan.

"I yield," My voice was strong, yet winded.

I was jerked to my feet. There was a snap as weight was put on it. My ankle screamed in protest, causing my leg to buckle. I flinched but did my best to not show it. I wouldn't show weakness while under the scrutiny of my enemies. They dragged me to a horse after tying my hands together behind my back. They tossed me over the back of it.

My breath was knocked out of me, and blood rushed to my head as I hung over the horse, head down. When the horse took off in a gallop, I counted myself lucky that I wasn't being forced to follow the horse. I wouldn't have been able to walk behind. I was certain my ankle was broken. The pain radiating from it was a good indication of that. Closing my eyes, I willed the nausea to subside so I wouldn't vomit all over the horse. As much as I didn't care about the rider and wished him dead, the animal was innocent.

I wasn't sure how long we had been moving, but the rain had let up some time ago. My head was aching and spinning from being slung over the horse as long as I had been. Gratitude washed through me when the horse stopped, indicating that we had made it to our destination.

Someone grabbed the back of my shirt and yanked me backward off the horse. I landed on my feet, the broken ankle giving out on me. I hit the ground with a gasp. It took several breaths to overcome the pain. I wasn't given a chance to recover from it before I was yanked up by the hair and shoved forward.

I limped and staggered as much as possible to keep from hitting the ground again. I wasn't about to give them something to laugh about by falling yet again. As much as it hurt, I was able to keep upright. I followed with only a little encouragement from the soldier behind me, and his sword. If I slowed, I felt the blade push into my back to keep me moving.

They took me directly to a cell, not giving me a chance to look around. Once I was locked in, I heard voices on the other side of the heavy wooden door.

"Do ye' think Zeus will do as the master wishes?"

"If he wants the Valkyrie, he will. I've heard that he is willing to give plenty of gold and goods to get the broad. She embarrassed him in front of his court and family. He can't let that go." the other voice said with humor lacing his voice. "Between us, I would have loved to see that. I heard that she made quite the show and made him out to be the jester in his own court."

"Aye. I also heard that she disrespected him as she left. Complete disregard for the Greek ways."

A third voice, feminine, came into the mix. "You two goons are clucking like hens. And they say ladies are the gossips. I think that the Valkyrie was brave for standing up to him. I almost feel bad for her. To be slain for standing up for her beliefs. 'Tis sad. Now you two hens go on and get the gallows ready. The master insists on an old-fashioned hanging."

Once the voices faded and footsteps disappeared, I pulled my legs onto the pallet that was on the floor for me and removed my boot. My ankle was three times its normal size and an ugly shade of purple. It was almost black. I could see where the bones were out of place.

I closed my eyes for a moment and took a deep breath. Quickly, I grabbed my foot and shifted my leg, forcing my ankle to go back into place. I couldn't hold back the cry of pain. My chest heaved from the pain shooting through my body. Tears and pain racked through me. I calmed myself before gently putting my boot back on, tightening the lacings to try to immobilize my ankle.

Once it was set, I wondered why I had just put myself through all that pain. I was going to die anyway. I closed my eyes, deciding I was going to rest before they came back for me.

Chapter 18

It wasn't long before they came back for me. They had seven guards bringing me to my execution. Two took me by the arms and one covered my face with a burlap sack. The sack smelled of bad breath, sweat, and tears. I figured it was the same one used for more than one hanging. I hoped that it wasn't going to be over my head as I died. I wanted to see the sky as life drained out of me.

My ankle throbbed and screamed while we walked. I bit my lower lip, trying to keep the pain at bay. I wasn't going to have much longer to worry about it. They were going to kill me as soon as we got where we were going. I wasn't going to show weakness or fear in my last minutes alive.

As I thought about death, I hoped my mother would be there to greet me on the other side. I had a half second of questioning if there was even another side left to go to. I was about to find out.

I could tell we were back outside when the breeze brushed across my legs. I wondered if we would be walking much further. My ankle wasn't going to hold my weight much longer. The pain was excruciating.

"Step up," the guard holding my left arm instructed.

Instead of letting myself fall and make a spectacle of myself before my death, I did as I was told. They led me for what seemed an eternity before we stopped.

The rope was placed over my head and tightened so it wouldn't slip when the time came for me to die.

"Remove the covering. I want to see the face of the one who thought she would get away with speaking to me in such manner without consequence." A voice boomed. It was as loud as thunder rolling above my head.

One of the guards grabbed the sack and yanked it off my head, taking a handful of hair along with it. The pain was instantaneous and searing where it was jerked out. The sunlight was blinding once the sack was completely removed from my head.

I looked up to the sky, seeing clouds on the horizon. They were dark storm clouds that were moving in at a swift pace. I prayed they would make it before they pulled the lever. The storm would remind me of what I was dying for, whom I was dying for. The rain and thunder would bring me closer to my love, Thor.

I lowered my gaze to where the voice had come from. I made eye contact with the one and only Zeus. He was an intimidating presence; however, he was no Odin. I smiled and couldn't help but feel the joy that rushed through me as his smile disappeared.

"Do you have any last words?" he asked, leaning against the rail of the balcony.

"I do." My voice was confident and carried well. "It doesn't matter that you are going to kill me. The seed of rebellion among my people has been planted and they will rise up. The Valkyries are not ones to be held down. We were born to fight. That is what they will do. They just need to wake up and see what has happened. If I embarrassed you in any way, I will happily do it again."

"You insolent, wisp of a woman. You have no idea who you are dealing with. I will not tolerate such insolence." He turned slightly and made a motion with his hand.

To my horror, Loki stepped out of the shadows and smiled down at me, then turned his attention to the executioner. He nodded once. There was a clicking sound, then suddenly the floor dropped out from under me.

The rope jerked against my neck. All air had been knocked out of me. I struggled to get some air as the rope strangled me. There was a roaring, but I couldn't tell if it was the blood rushing through my head or the crowd.

I thought I heard a scream through the thundering, but I wouldn't swear to anything. Spots began to gather in my eyesight and the edges became dark. I continued to choke and gasp, trying to get air, to no avail.

Suddenly, I was on the ground, the rope loosened. I gasped in air as fast as I could. My throat and lungs burned as I greedily gulped in the precious life-giving oxygen. Hands gently pulled the rope over my head and cut the binding on my wrists.

I struggled to sit up, but gentle, yet firm hands stopped me from moving. "Easy, Kara. You have to give your body time to adjust to getting air again. Slowly. You're safe now."

My mind froze when I realized who the owner of the voice was. Mist. She was there, saving me. I had wanted to find her, I didn't realize that she would not only find me, but save me from meeting my maker, again.

My eyes met hers. She smiled and held a hand out to me. I placed my hand in hers, letting her help me to my feet. Her arm came around my waist, steadying me so I didn't topple over when my legs tried giving out. I was still weak from lack of oxygen. My head pounded. I didn't show any of the weakness. I stood there, waiting to see what was going to happen next.

"Kara will not die today. Not in my palace." Mist's voice echoed through the now silent courtyard. "She is now under my protection."

She led me out of the courtyard, back into the palace. We slowly, painstakingly, made our way up the marble staircase. My lungs burned and ached from trying to take in the air needed to climb the stairs. We had to stop frequently in order for me to catch my breath.

We didn't speak as we walked. There was much to discuss, but an open stairway was not the place to do it. I also didn't have the energy or the breath to carry on a conversation. The sting of betrayal washed through me again as I remembered her pushing me through the Rainbow Bridge with Loki by her side.

Finally, we reached the top of the stairs. My ankle screamed in protest as I continued to try to walk. I gave in and limped. The pain was starting to take over and I wasn't sure I was going to make it to our destination. I had no idea how far our destination was from where we were. I prayed that I would make it. I couldn't let myself give into defeat in front of anyone.

Mist stopped in front of a door and studied me for a moment before opening it and guiding me in. Her grip on my waist had tightened and she lifted, taking some of the pressure off my abused ankle.

"Been a hundred years and you are still a stubborn ass," she remarked as she led me to the bed and helped me sit. "You could have said that you were injured."

Anger flared in me. "When did I have time to mention my injuries, eh? When I was dangling from that rope, having the life strangled out of me? Or while we were in front of that crowd of people including those who wish to see me dead. That would have been a good time to say something. Or while I was fighting to get air back into my body, so I didn't die."

"Aye, any of those times would have been great. Or you could have mentioned it as I made you walk up those stairs. I could have helped you more if I had known." She hugged me, surprising me after the hostility I had shown her and the anger that had been returned. "Kara, I am pleased to see you are still alive. I prayed to Odin that you would survive the trip to Midgard. Then, when I heard of the Valkyrie that stood up to Zeus, I knew it had to be you."

"Did you know I was being held prisoner?" Doubt that her words were sincere made its way into my mind. "How could you betray us like you did, Mist? I trusted you and you stabbed me in the back."

I could feel tears building in the back of my eyes. I blinked rapidly, trying to fight them back. I wouldn't show her how much she truly hurt me. I hoped she thought that the betrayal against the Valkyries was what I spoke in reference to.

"I didn't betray you. I saved you. If I hadn't made you go through the bridge, you would have stayed and died there. Surtr had already destroyed much of Asgard and was approaching the Bi-Frost quickly. I couldn't see you die like the others. I knew that Loki would save me."

"You chose Loki over your sisters! Loki is the enemy. He helped orchestrate Ragnarök and brought

147

Hel's army to Asgard to destroy us. He watched in glee as Odin was killed."

"You know not of what he had planned. I didn't choose Loki over you. I chose love. My love for my sisters is equal to my love for Loki, but different. I saved you; I did what I could to save everyone from Ragnarök. I didn't let Loki kill Thor, now did I? Loki had promised me that you wouldn't die, he would help save you from Surtr and yourself if need be. He knows how stubborn you are as well."

She took a deep breath and paced the room. When she returned to the foot of the bed, she exhaled and continued. "He is out there right now, cleaning up my mess of saving you. I just went against the gods by letting you live and putting you under my protection. He offered to let the hanging happen here, in fact he insisted on it to make sure that if it were you they were going to kill, that he could keep his promise and help me save you. The knot wasn't tied properly, or it would have snapped your neck as the floor dropped from beneath you. You owe Loki gratitude, not condemnation."

I stared at her, unsure of what to say to the revelations. Loki had killed Thor's brother. He had helped with the destruction of Asgard. How could he have been helping as well? That didn't make sense. He was a foe, not a friend.

"You can believe me or not, that is up to you. But by Odin's beard, I will take care of you and tend your wounds. After you are healed to my satisfaction, we will discuss the next steps of your plan. If you trust me to, that is." She didn't give me a chance to respond before she grabbed my leg and began to undo the boot. She yanked it off, none-too-gently and dropped it with a thud on the floor.

I winced as pain shot through my ankle and up my leg when she pulled the boot off. I was tempted to kick her in the face with my good leg, but I rethought that since she had a firm grip on my foot. I didn't need to end up with more injuries than what I already had. Instead, I looked down at my ankle to see that it was swollen twice the size it had been and the coloring of it was now black, purple, and green. My ankle looked like if I were to prick it, it would explode.

Mist stood up and went to the door, opening it a crack. I could hear her speaking in soft murmurs, but I was unable to decipher what she had said. She came back and knelt on the floor at the foot of the bed.

"I need some supplies before I can tend to your ankle. I am sure that you broke the bone, but it looks like you did well enough setting it. I am going to have to reset it just to be sure. Worry not, we have some of the best healers in the land here. You will be back on your feet in no time."

"I need to go now. I have things to do." I struggled to sit up, but she pushed me back with one hand to my shoulder.

"Don't make me strap you down to this bed." From the look on her face, I believed she would.

The healers chose that time to enter the room in a frenzy of movement. There were three of them and they moved with grace I had never seen. They were doing different things to prepare their work, but it was almost as if they moved as one.

One of them stood off to the side, mixing something. When she turned, she had a cup in her hand. She held it out to me and spoke. Her voice was as light as air. If I hadn't seen her lips move, I wouldn't have been sure she had even spoken. "Drink this. It will ease your pain and help you rest so you may heal."

I stared at the contents of the cup. It was purple and had a swirl of light dancing through it. I didn't want to drink it. It was pretty, but I was certain it would taste horrible. I attempted to hand it back to the healer.

"If ye don't drink it on your own, I will pour it down your throat," Mist growled. One look into her eyes told me she would do exactly that.

Reluctantly, I drank the purple contents of the cup. I couldn't identify what it tasted like either. It actually tasted like nothing. Not even the hint of a water taste. I finished off the cup and handed it back to the healer, who whisked it away.

I could feel my heartbeat in my chest. It took four thumps for the concoction to kick in. My eyes drooped, and I felt myself drift off into a healing sleep.

CHAPTER 19

Gradually, I became aware of my surroundings. There was no noise except the slight creaking of a wooden floor. Opening my eyes, I looked around to see that I was still on the bed Mist had helped me into. Sitting up, I glanced down at my leg to see that it was wrapped from foot to knee. They had some kind of immobilizer to keep it from moving. It was uncomfortable, but it didn't hurt.

My eyes traveled the room, settling on a rocking chair in the corner. That had to be what was making the creaking noise. Mist sat in the chair, slowly rocking it back and forth, eyes on me. When my eyes met hers, she smiled at me.

"Rise and shine," Her voice was light, but strained.

"What happened?" I tensed as I prepared for the worst.

"Nothing. I had hoped that you would sleep longer, so you could heal more, but I should have known better. You never do what I expect or need you to do, unless it's in battle."

I studied her eyes and could see shadows in them. She was worried about something. "Mist, what is worrying you?"

"Zeus didn't take the news that you were under our protection well. Which we expected. He has now put our kingdom under siege. My people are going to starve unless we hand you over to him. I refuse to do so, now we have to come up with a plan to keep food in the bellies of my people."

"I will go with him. No need to harm innocents in the process. This is my battle, not yours. I appreciate you saving my life, but I'll go."

"No. Not happening. Loki and the commanders are working on a plan to strike back. All will be well soon enough. You'll just have to stay here a little longer."

"I can't. I have to get back. I had injured people with me when I was taken captive. They were hiding and I've got to get to them and make sure they are safe."

"Where were you heading? I haven't heard of anyone else being captured, so I believe that your friends are safe."

"Are you?"

"Am I what?"

"Safe." I stared at her, trying to see the Mist I had grown up with and loved in the woman before me. She looked the same, yet her eyes were different. The war had affected everyone. If I were honest with myself, I had nightmares, but I wouldn't admit it, even to me.

She nodded once. "I am. Loki would never hurt me. Please, Kara, let me explain what happened."

I wanted to tell her to shut up. I didn't need to know how she betrayed us, yet there was a voice deep within me that needed to know her story. I wanted to know what happened. How she could have been tangled up with the enemy.

"Loki was supposed to be the enemy, yet he had always been kind to me. I know how he treated you, but it is his nature. He wouldn't have hurt you. When we first met, truly met, it was shortly before they found Baldr dead. We met on Midgard. I didn't know it was Loki until later. The way he looked at me was magic. We instantly fell in love. It's hard to explain, hard to understand. I still don't get it myself. He had asked me to run away with him and I agreed. I tried to convince him to stop with Ragnarök, but he couldn't. Everything had already been set in motion, stopping it wasn't an option. That was when he agreed to save you."

"I didn't ask for him to save me."

"I know you didn't, I did. I couldn't let my best friend, my sister, die in that wretched war. I know what our oath was and that we were all willing to die, but I couldn't help myself. It wasn't necessary for you to die. Damn it, Kara! Why do you have to make things so difficult?"

"I'm not." I crossed my arms. "You let our sisters die. The ones that didn't were imprisoned and you let that continue. How is that me being difficult? You made your choices, Mist. Now you have to live with them. I've made mine as well. I am going to do what is necessary to save our sisters, free them."

"I want to help you with that. When we first arrived here, I didn't know what happened to them. I thought they had made it safely and were building a home. How was I supposed to know they were being made slaves? When we found out, it was as we were settling into our land. Then we decided that we needed to become stronger and more secure in our holdings before taking on New Olympus. We have saved some. If we have gotten a refugee or escapee, we have taken them in and gave them sanctuary. We are not the enemy, Kara."

"Are you not?" I climbed out of the bed, wincing when I put weight on my ankle. It wasn't as painful as it had been before, which was a great improvement. I was grateful for the work the healers had done on me.

"No, I'm not. You never thought that before."

"You never betrayed me before."

"Kara, we aren't going to see eye to eye on this. I love you. You are my sister. I am going to do everything I can to save you, even if I have to save you from yourself."

I cocked an eyebrow at her. "You can try."

A smile tugged at her lips. I could see her struggling to contain it. It was typical of Mist to be entertained by a serious moment. I sighed and limped to the window. The courtyard was abandoned except for the guards that were either standing at attention or making rounds. There were more guards at the gate and along the walls.

The situation ran through my head. Mist's people were in trouble because of me, yet she refused to hand me over which would solve her problems. There was a siege underway, which hadn't been done since before the age of technology in Midgard, which was now a thing of the past. I supposed the saying that history repeated itself was correct.

I turned and looked at Mist. She was still sitting in the rocking chair; she hadn't moved. If I didn't know any better, I would have believed that she wasn't fazed by our words. Her eyes gave her away though. They always gave her away. It was her tell.

"We need to get word out to Thor. He would come and help. Let's send a message to him."

"Kara, when are you going to understand that sending word to Thor won't do any good? Loki is his enemy now. He blames him for your death. Well, your supposed death. He blames him for everything. I don't believe there will ever be peace between them again. He won't do anything to help. Besides, there is no way to get the word out. We're under siege, remember?"

I growled in frustration. "Aye, I remember. But I have to do something. I can't let your people suffer due to my presence. A Valkyrie protects and that isn't protecting. I feel as if I am hiding. It feels cowardly."

She stood and crossed the room to me then. "It isn't cowardly. You are doing what needs to be done for you. It's okay for you to care for yourself."

"Not at the expense of others. I'll leave here and they will follow me. Please don't argue with me any longer. It grows tiresome. I am leaving at dusk. Do you know a way out that will give me a lead on them?"

She looked away before she answered me. "One. You can go through the tunnels that lead from the dungeon. They open up in the Forest of Illusion, but you must be careful. The forest will try to turn you around and lure you into traps of your own making. It isn't safe."

"I don't have a choice. Don't fret. I'll be fine. It isn't the first time I've gone against my own thoughts. You are your most dangerous enemy. You never know when it will sneak up against you."

"Kara, I don't think—"

"Mist," I cut her off. "It's settled. I know you care about me, as I care for you, but I'm not a child anymore. I'm a Valkyrie and a warrior. I'm leaving as soon as the sun sets for the evening. Then you can tell Zeus that I am no longer here and to call off the siege. He will come after me and leave you be. Hopefully,

I'll make it to Thunder Valley and Thor before Zeus catches up to me."

She hugged me tightly. "Stay safe, sister. I don't want to lose you again. I will have the kitchen pack provisions for you, so you don't starve on your journey."

"Thank you, but make sure the pack is light. My ankle still isn't healed yet, and I don't need the extra weight."

"How about I have a horse prepared for you as well? It will make your travels faster."

I shook my head no. "Too much noise, but thank you. The journey will be best done on foot."

She nodded. "I will go prepare. You should rest as much as you can this day so you will have plenty of energy to leave. Rest your mind, make sure it is clear before you go into the forest. I fear for you if it isn't."

I watched her go as she left the room. A part of me wanted to give her a hug and beg her to go with me, but I knew she wouldn't. The other part of me never wanted to see her again. I still felt the sting of betrayal when I looked at her. It made me want to weep, but I didn't have time for it.

Mist was right that I needed to rest and clear my head. Exhaustion was already beating at me, and I had only been up for a short while. I limped back to the bed and fell face first on it. Sleep overcame me before I could move and lie on the bed correctly.

CHAPTER 20

Opening one eye, I realized it was dark. I sat up, struggling to open both of my eyes. My eyelids were still heavy. The room was dark, and the curtains were drawn shut. I climbed out of bed and made my way to the window. Pulling open the heavy drapes, I saw that the sun was beginning to set. It was time for me to go.

Once ready, I grabbed the pack that Mist left me. There was a walking stick leaning on the wall next to the chair. I grabbed it as well so I could steady myself on my journey.

As I walked down the hallway, I was met by a guard. He gave me a slight nod, indicating that I should follow him. I figured it was something that Mist had come up with so I would be able to find my way out without just aimlessly wandering around the castle.

We walked down several flights of stairs. Once we were in the grand hall, he led me out of the castle to another building. There, we descended more stairs until we were in the dungeons. I could hear people crying and begging for freedom.

It sounded like there were women and children in the dungeons as well as the men. The crying broke my heart and I wanted to free them all. The guard glanced at me from the corner of his eye. Something on my face must have told him what I was thinking because he reached out and took my arm to guide me through the dungeon. It would have been easy to break free of his grip, but I knew what his intention was, so I let him lead me. It wasn't the time to start a fight with Loki, but I would see to it that the children were freed.

It mattered not what the adults did, the children were innocent.

Once at the tunnels, the guard stopped and turned to me. "This is as far as I was told to bring you. The rest of the journey, you will be alone. Follow this tunnel. No matter what you hear or see, continue forward until you get to the fork. Then head right, it will take you straight out into the forest."

He left me alone in the tunnel. I didn't hesitate though. I just started walking through the darkness. It was eerie, yet the further I went, the calmer I felt.

I had been walking for quite some time, I couldn't determine the exact amount in the dark, when the noises started to sound. There were echoes and cries for help. The sounds reminded me of the battles and deaths at Asgard. The screams were those of agony. My heart broke as the lives ended around me.

I kept walking. The guard's advice ran through my head with every step that I took. *Don't look back. Stay on the path. It is all in my head. I hope it's all in my head. Stop it! It is. Keep going. You have to get out of here.*

I pushed myself forward until I came to the fork in the tunnel. One side led to the left, the other right. I hesitated for a moment, trying to remember which direction I was supposed to go. As I studied the two tunnels, I thought I saw something flash in the one heading left. That was when I remembered I was supposed to go right. I was curious, but now wasn't the time to go getting into trouble or lost. I went right.

When the tunnel opened into the forest, the night had completely settled in. I took a deep breath of fresh air. It smelled of dew and dirt. I kept walking, knowing I had to be as far from the kingdom as I could before sunrise. I would be able to rest when I reached my destination.

The sun was just starting to rise when I reached the end of the woods. There was a horse tethered to a tree. It pulled on its reigns, trying to free itself. The horse was magnificent and reminded me of mine at home.

I approached the animal, my free hand extended to give it a chance to smell me before I got any closer. I spoke gently, trying to soothe the beast. "It's okay. I'm not going to hurt you. Such a pretty girl. Calm. There you go."

As the horse settled, I approached and tentatively reached out to stroke the horse's long nose. The horse snorted at me but seemed to approve of my touch.

I looked around the area, searching for the owner. I would have never just left my horse stuck on a branch, unable to fend for itself or get any water.

"Well, we are truly alone. You will have to go with me then. Do you think you can give me a ride to Thunder Valley and Thor?"

The horse bobbed its head.

I untied the tether and mounted the horse. Since I wasn't walking, I didn't need the stick, so I let it fall uselessly to the ground. I turned the horse around and began to ride, slowly building up speed until she was running at a full gallop.

She didn't stop until we were in front of the gates of Thunder Valley. I stared at it for several moments while I was flooded with emotions. I wanted to run in there and jump into Thor's arms, yet I knew we had work to do. Another part of me wanted to turn and head back the other direction because I feared seeing him again. I hadn't seen him in over a hundred years.

I didn't believe the stories that he mourned for me still and that his love never died. He had probably moved on and found another wife. One that would be meekly by his side.

Kara! I mentally scolded myself. *Now is not the time to pity yourself. You need his help. Go through the gate and do what needs to be done. You can deal with emotions later.*

I took a deep breath and slowly guided the horse through the gate.

CHAPTER 21

As soon as we were inside the walls, we were surrounded by armed guards. I sighed. This was going to end in one of two ways. Either I was going to kill them all or they were going to kill me. All I knew was I wasn't going to go down without a fight.

"Stand down and we won't kill you!" one of the guards shouted.

"You stand down. You see I come unarmed." I didn't shout, but my voice was carried by the wind. "I am here to see Thor."

"No one sees the king. He wishes to not be disturbed." the guard shouted again.

"No need to shout. I can hear perfectly fine. I repeat, I must see Thor immediately. I am his wife."

There was a mixed reaction in the growing crowd that surrounded us. Gasps and mumbles echoed around us. I stood straight and waited for the guards to let me pass.

"Lies! Our queen died during Ragnarök." The guard that had been speaking pushed through the crowd to tower over me. "You dare insult our intelligence!"

I puffed my chest out and squared my shoulders. "You insult your queen. Now let me pass."

The blow to the back of my head was sudden and unexpected. The ground met with my face and my legs gave out from under me.

***

When I came to, the first thing I heard was the all too familiar sounds of a dungeon. I groaned and sat up. I had been placed on a cot in a cell, which was an upgrade from the cell I had been in while I was captive at Hourglass City.

I stood, wincing as my ankle reminded me it wasn't fully healed and hurt like a bitch. I took a few deep breaths, trying to breathe through the pain. Once I was able to push it from my mind, I paced the cell. I wondered how long it would take for them to come get me or execute me.

The thought of my execution made me scream. I was getting tired of constantly fighting my impending demise. I was also tired of constantly being locked up. That scream was followed by another, then another. I screamed until my throat burned and was raw from the action.

"Shut up, damn woman!" one of the guards yelled down the hall at me.

"Come down here and make me," I rasped out.

"I just may."

I hoped that he would since I knew I was able to kick the guard's ass. It would make me feel better to beat someone down. The sound of footsteps echoing down the corridor toward me made me smile. He was going to come down and try to make me. I couldn't wait. My heart began pounding in my chest. Blood thundered in my ears in anticipation of the fight.

The guard opened the door of the cell and stepped in. He walked up to me, not even bothering to make sure that the door was closed behind him. He towered over me and slowly reached out at me.

I ducked, swinging my leg out, knocking his out from under him. The guard landed on the ground with a thud. Without giving him time to catch his breath, I attacked. My foot connected with his face, and I heard the crunch of his nose.

Jumping over him, I raced out of the cell, grabbing the door and pulling it shut behind me. As soon as I knew that it was latched, I took off running through the corridor toward the stairs. Bounding upward, I braced as I reached the door. I didn't chance stopping, just slammed my shoulder into it. Luckily, the door wasn't locked, and it swung open effortlessly. At the top of the stairs, I stopped and looked around, trying to figure out which way to go.

My instincts were screaming for me to go left, so I did. My luck came to an end there though. As I pushed through a second door, I was overtaken by the guard. They appeared out of nowhere, surrounding me. I tried to fight my way through the guards, but it was useless.

Someone grabbed my hair, jerking me backwards. An arm went across my shoulders, a dagger dug into my neck.

"If you move or try to fight me, I'll slit your throat," the voice that belonged to the arm whispered in my ear.

I could smell his breath, which was vile, but I stayed still because I believed him. The tone he had used had been laced with threat. And promise. "I won't move, but please stop breathing on me. A troll would have better smelling breath than you."

"I should just do it and be done with it," the guard threatened, pushing the knife a little harder into my throat.

"You do that, and you'll be executed immediately," another guard warned. "You know the rules. We must take her to him."

They led me through the halls, digging the knife into my throat to keep me from fighting or trying to get away from him. I stumbled a little from my sore ankle. The tip of the dagger jabbed into my throat a little deep, breaking the skin. I felt the trickle of blood running down my neck.

I was taken to the Great Hall. Once we reached the steps, the guard moved the dagger and shoved me. I stumbled to the floor, barely catching myself with my hands before my face met the marble.

"So, this is the lass that has been causing so much trouble?" a familiar voice asked from above me. "Seems small compared to the stories I've been hearing around here. Stand, woman."

I raised my head just high enough to see the boots of the man speaking. Slowly, my eyes raised up the length of his body until my eyes met his. It was the one and only Thor.

His eyes widened for a moment, then darkened. There was a roll of thunder outside. Waves of anger rolled off him and almost smothered me.

"What magic is this!?" he demanded, looking around. "Has Loki entered my territory, pulling tricks on me?"

When no one answered him, thunder crashed outside, loud enough that it almost felt like the palace rumbled.

"Answer me!" he bellowed.

"What magic?" I asked softly. "I know of no magic."

He walked down the steps of the dais and squatted so that he was eye level with me. "There is only one way that I would see this face again. It has to be magic."

I slowly shook my head no. "There is no magic. At least not here. I am not magic."

Thor reached his hand out like he was going to touch me, but he stopped inches from my face. "I wish to touch you, but I'm afraid."

"Of what?" I asked quietly.

"That if I touch you, you will disappear like you have so many times over the past century."

I raised up, gently putting my hands on top of his. "I'm not going to disappear. I'm here, Thor."

He helped me stand, then cupped my face. "Kara? Are you truly here?"

"Truly." I whispered.

He brought his mouth down to mine and kissed me gently on the lips. Feelings and emotions I hadn't felt in a long time washed over me. I threw my arms around his neck and hugged him tightly. His arms wrapped around me in return.

"I've missed you so," he whispered in my hair.

"I was afraid you'd forgotten about me." I murmured back.

"Never."

He brought his lips back to mine in a kiss that made me light-headed. I broke the kiss, resting my forehead on his. I had my eyes closed while I tried to control my breathing. The feeling of home washed over me.

It took me several long moments for me to be able to remind myself why I was there. I had to keep my mind on the goal and objective. It wasn't the time for me to break down and forget my obligations. I took a deep, controlling breath and stepped out of the safety of his arms.

"Thor, I must speak with you." I felt my nerves buzzing as I stared into his beautiful face. I studied his face while he seemed to struggle with the distance. He didn't look different even though it had been a hundred years since I saw him. The only difference was the shadows under his eyes.

"You may speak freely, Kara. You know this."

"Did you know the other Valkyries have been imprisoned by the god named Zeus?"

The tightness around his eyes and shoulders told me he had been aware of it. I felt anger grow in my stomach. I wanted to punch him. He had known and did nothing to help. The anger washed away as quickly as it flared. It was replaced by disappointment and sadness. He wasn't the same man that I had married.

He looked over my head and spoke. "Clear the room. I need to speak in private with my wife."

As soon as the doors closed with the last of the people that had been in the room, he turned away from me and walked to the window. I watched him, waiting. I knew he was likely gathering his thoughts before he spoke. He stared out the window before sighing.

"I have heard such rumblings." When he spoke, his voice was soft, almost distant. "You do not understand what this past century without you has done to me. I have been lost, hurt, broken. Nothing has mattered to me since arriving to Midgard without you. My heart was gone."

"You didn't protect our people." Disappointment was thick in my voice and almost choked me. "You aren't the man that I married. I've got to go. I promised them, I need to free them."

I turned and walked to the door, heartbroken. This wasn't the way I expected out reunion to go. I had hoped that he had been planning on finding a way to free them. I walked to the door and reached my hand out to grab the handle.

"Do not take another step!" He roared. Thunder blasted through the room. He strode toward me in angry steps. Grabbing my shoulder, he turned me so I was facing him. His face was flushed with anger. He pushed my shoulders back so I was pressed against the door. When he spoke again, his voice was a low growl. "When I made it to Midgard, I barely lived. Darkness and fever had taken me over for more than a week while I healed. When I found out what happened, I was beside myself. Then I had to work on making a home for those that I knew survived. From all appearances and what I had heard, you were dead. I was told you stayed behind in Asgard to close the bridge. There was no talk of you surviving. I searched for you for decades to no avail. There was no hint that you were alive. I didn't give up, but I couldn't continue to neglect the people."

His pain radiated through me, making my chest hurt. I could see it shining in his eyes as he watched me, willing me to understand. I struggled with the idea that he almost didn't survive. Fever was dangerous, even for gods. While it wouldn't have likely taken him to Helgard; there could have been damage to his brain and other effects.

"What about the Valkyries?" I asked. "You let them be enslaved for a century. You did nothing to help."

"My love, it takes time to build a secure, stable empire. I had to round up enough warriors that would be suitable to be guard and army. The Valkyries that I did have with me have been helping the warriors train. We needed to become strong before I broached the subject of freeing them. Give me time. I will petition Zeus for their release." He reached up with a shaky hand and cupped my face.

"You are?" I felt hope build in my chest.

"Yes. We will release them together."

CHAPTER 22

"How dare he refuse my messenger!" Thor thundered as he paced the room. "That arrogant, selfish prick."

"What do you wish to do next?" I asked, watching him. He stopped and turned toward me.

"Next, I go visit the arrogant ass."

"We."

He cocked an eyebrow. "We?"

I stood and walked to him. "Yes. We. I am going with you. If you think that you are going alone, you must rethink. I'm going with you. We've been apart too long. May I ask you something?"

"Of course."

"I sent friends ahead. Long story. But I haven't seen them since I arrived. Did they make it here?"

His brows furrowed. "I don't recall anyone announced, but they aren't always announced to me."

"Brynhild and Sanngrid were among those who would have arrived. The others were a bit, uh, different." Anxiety rose in me. I wouldn't be able to forgive myself if something happened to them. "The others of the party were a unicorn, gnome, and centaur."

"Really? Now I must check with the guard. I don't remember anything unorthodox coming to my palace."

He walked to the door and opened it a crack. He shut it then returned to my side. When the door opened seconds later, I stiffened as the guard I had tangled with walked in. His eyes shot daggers at me, but he didn't speak or acknowledge me in any other way.

"My lord," He bowed deeply.

"Did we have a centaur with Valkyries arrive at the gate this past fortnite?"

"We did, Sire. The injured Valkyries were taken to the infirmary while the others were put in holding cells."

Anger washed over me so suddenly it felt like I was going to drown. "Do you have a habit of not telling your king that there are visitors? You just arrest them, assuming what? They are just here to start trouble. Mayhap they were seeking asylum and you imprisoned them. You stupid oaf!"

Thor's hand on my arm kept me from moving, or I would have likely struck the guard.

"Why was I not made aware of the situation? Where are the Valkyries and the others now?"

The guard bowed again. "Your solitude is important to you. We didn't feel it pressing to inform you about some trespassers--"

"Trespassers?" I interrupted. "Did you give them a chance to ask for help?"

"Kara," Thor said, softly squeezing my hand. "I shall ask the questions."

I bit my lip from saying something that I would probably regret. This was getting tiresome.

"When was it decided that I was not to be informed on what was going on in my own territory? I don't remember giving that command." Before the guard could speak, Thor held up his hand. "You are relieved of your duties. I will assemble the guard together and choose a new captain since you are unable to make wise choices. I wish you gone by sunrise, or you will spend time in the cells."

The guard bowed and slowly backed out of the room. Once we were alone again, I turned toward Thor.

"What do we do now?" I was furious and wanted to kill something.

"We go find your friends. Let's start at the infirmary, since we are certain that's where two were taken. Maybe they are still there."

I followed him out the door as he led the way to the infirmary. As we walked, I was able to see little snippets of the palace. I wouldn't have been able to find my way through it by myself; of that, I was certain. From what I could see, it was bigger than the Palace at Asgard. He led me to a marble staircase and headed down.

We stepped off at a landing, turned down a hallway, and went through a door. Once inside, we stopped. The room was stark white with curtains placed strategically around the room, blocking the views of the beds. The beds were lined against the walls like bunks. Most of the curtains were open, giving us a clear view of the room.

A healer walked into the room holding a vile and syringe. When she saw us, she froze, eyes widening. "My lord, is there something I can help you with?"

"We are looking for the Valkyries that were admitted a couple days ago." He stepped toward her, voice gentle.

"Aye. Follow me. I was just about to treat the thin one. They are very dehydrated and malnourished, but we've been working on that along with external injuries that are apparent." She filled the syringe and checked the level before continuing. "I'm worried about the mental trauma of being held as a slave, but we won't know how much they were affected until they wake. We've been keeping the one, Sanngrid, I believe, sedated and the other hasn't woke up since she's been here."

"Is Brynhild going to be alright?" I asked around the lump forming in my throat. I couldn't bear the thought of her not being well. We hadn't seen eye to eye for most of my life, but I couldn't picture life without her. She was family, as were all the Valkyries.

The nurse fidgeted like the question made her anxious. It took her several long moments before she answered. "If she can overcome the dehydration and physical damage, she should wake up. I'm not trying to wake her because she needs healing that she only gets from sleeping."

"Send for me immediately when she wakes." I said stiffly.

Thor squeezed my arm in a reassuring manner. "Yes, inform us as soon as there are any changes in their condition. This is my wife, your queen, Kara."

The nurse gave us a nod of acknowledgement. She went through the curtain, needle in hand. When she came back out, her hands were empty. She nodded again and headed toward the door she had appeared from.

"Wait." I held out a hand to stop her.

"Yes?"

"May I see them?" I knew the request seemed silly, but in that moment, I felt it imperative that I see the two warriors.

She nodded and quietly left the room, giving us a moment to ourselves.

Once alone, I approached the first curtain. It was the one to which she had taken the needle. I slid it open a little and stepped inside the space.

Lying listlessly on the bed was Sanngrid. I stepped up to the side of the bed, gently placing my hand upon hers. She had bruises all over her body and she was so thin you could see her ribs through her hospital gown. Her cheeks were hollowed, and eyes shadowed. My eyes stopped at her neck where she bore wounds from wearing the collar and chains she'd had on. My heart ached for her and the pain she must have been in.

"I'm so sorry that you are here. I will do everything I can to avenge you," I whispered and kissed her forehead before walking away from her bed and approaching Brynhild's. When I saw her in the bed, my heart stopped. She looked small and weak. I had never seen Brynhild look that way. Valkyries were strong. I gave her hand a slight squeeze and felt a squeeze in return.

I returned to Thor's side and looked up at him. "Now we find the others."

A deadly calm washed over me. My vision was edged with red. I needed to kill something and was itching for a fight.

Thor turned me so I faced him. "I know what you are thinking, Kara. I can see it in your eyes. I feel it within myself as well, but there is nothing we can do yet. We must confront the enemy in person before we fight. We must give them a chance to secede."

I gave him a curt nod and turned so he could lead the way to the dungeons. As I followed him down, I had a feeling of discontentment wash over me. I hated dungeons, cells, prisons. The idea of being there again made me feel uneasy. It was probably from spending as much time as I had in them.

Once in the dungeon, I could hear voices all around. I peeked in the different cells, walking through. I didn't recognize the people as I checked. Once we got to the very last stall, there was a clicking noise that reminded me of hooves on stone. I looked into the cell to see Casos, a heavy manacle around his neck. He had shackles around his back legs, keeping him from moving away from the wall. His hands were shackled together.

"Thor, down here." I called, then turned my attention back to Casos. "Hang on, Casos. We will get you out of there. I'm so sorry about this. You should have never been arrested."

Casos stared at me for several heartbeats through the bars. It seemed like it took him a moment to recognize me. Then he looked away.

Thor approached, no key in hand. He grabbed the bars and yanked, pulling the door from the wall. There was a creak and a crack as the door came away in his hands. I rushed past him into the room and approached the centaur ahead of me.

Thor released Casos. I watched as the centaur rubbed his wrists then shoulders as the manacles fell away.

"Thank you for releasing me. We need to find Octavious. I heard him shouting earlier. I fear that his mouth will get him beheaded." he spoke softly, his voice hoarse. It sounded like he hadn't had water in a while.

"We will. We are also going to get Crimson out of here too." I promised.

He nodded, then his eyes shot to Thor. There was something in them that looked like resentment. I didn't blame him, but he had to know that it wasn't Thor's fault they had been imprisoned.

"What happened?" I asked, directing his attention back to me.

"When we entered the grounds, the Valkyries were taken from us forcefully and we were corralled like animals at spear and sword point. Octavious was clobbered on the head and stuffed in a burlap sack. Crimson immediately dropped to her knees and cooperated with the guard, instructing us to do the same. I was brought here and treated worse than an animal."

"You have my sincerest apologies," Thor bowed, speaking for the first time. "I was unaware of how guests were being treated when they entered my land. I have rectified the situation and hope you will indeed accept my apologies and extended hospitality."

Casos scoffed before he spoke. "We will discuss this again once we have Octavious and Crimson at my side. There is more than just I that deserve your apology, God of Thunder."

"That is fair. You will all receive my most sincere apologies."

We left the cell and went on the search for Crimson and Octavious. I stopped in the middle of the hallway, knowing that searching each cell would be time consuming. The hallway split into two directions, and I wasn't sure what was down each.

"Crimson!" I shouted. "If you can hear me, call out."

"Down here." The voice was faint and coming from the left side of the hall. We took off toward the direction of her voice. A hand came out between the bars of one of the cells. It was slender and pale. The skin was marred with bruises and discoloration that told of rough treatment.

As soon as she was released, I put my arms around her in an embrace. She returned it, but with a lot less strength.

"Are you well?" I asked, feeling concern pounding in my chest. It hurt to know that she was imprisoned for helping me. It hurt more, knowing that she had been mistreated. I examined the bruising on her face and neck. Another thought occurred to me. "Have you been violated?"

"No, my dear. I was treated with some dignity. I shall be fine. Just bumps and bruises."

I nodded. If she had been forced upon, heads were going to roll, so Thor's men were lucky. I would have killed every single one of them if they had laid a finger on her. Her safety was of utmost importance to me.

She followed me out of the cell. Stopping with the rest of the group, I looked at Thor.

"Where would the guards keep a gnome?" I asked.

Thor frowned while he thought about that. "I'm not entirely certain. I've never seen a gnome."

"Let us look then." I turned and walked away in search of Octavious.

We returned to the split passageway and stopped. I was starting to think maybe they killed him instead of imprisoning him.

"Thor, would they have killed him?" I asked softly.

Thor shook his head no. "Prisoners aren't to be executed without my permission."

"Yeah, well your guard wasn't too great at following your laws as is. They were imprisoning travelers for coming onto the land without your knowledge."

"Don't remind me." Thor said through gritted teeth. "They wouldn't dare kill someone without my knowing. There is no way I wouldn't have heard the barest of whispers about an execution."

I was torn where to go look next when we heard an echo of a brash voice.

"Lemme outta here!" It shouted. "When I get through with the lot of yous, yous will be sorry that you messed with me. I oughta turn you into dust. If you think the ogres are bad, you haven't messed with us . . ."

"That would be Octavious," Crimson smiled. "He can be quite colorful."

We went down the other hallway, listening to the threats and curses as we came closer.

"I'll gut you and strangle you with your own insides. Then I'll put you on a spit and roast ya over open flames to feed you to the bugs."

Coming upon an open chamber, I looked around. The voice was loud now, indicating we were close. On the far side of the chamber, there was a burlap sack hanging from a hook over what looked to be a fire pit. The pit wasn't lit, but there was enough tinder to get a good flame going.

The burlap sack swung ferociously around in circles, the contents moving with effort. The voice was coming from it.

"I will cut bits off of you and throw it in the pond for the fishes, yet I doubt they will even take a nibble of the vileness that is you."

I rushed over and, with the help of Thor, I cut him down and released him from the sack. When

Octavious was released, he started swinging his fists wildly around at what he thought was the enemy.

"Octavious, tis us. Calm yourself." Casos scratched out. "Kara has arrived and is having us freed."

Slowly, Octavious stopped fighting the imaginary enemies and looked up at those of us in the room. Then he strode over to Thor and kicked him in the shin.

"Shit!" Thor bellowed, jumping back. "I have half a mind to smash your skull in."

"Try it, you overgrown hemorrhoid. Then you will see the wrath of Octavious the great." Octavious balled his hands in fists like he was ready to strike at any moment.

"Don't you mean, Octavious the tiny?" Thor asked, amusement flitting across his face.

"Enough." I stepped in between the two, stopping the likely brawl that would be coming. "We don't have time to squabble. Octavious, Thor is freeing you and begging for forgiveness for locking you up. And Thor, Octavious has the right to be angry. Your people had him tied in a sack, for Odin's sake."

They stared each other down before turning. The movement was simultaneous so neither saw my grin. They were destined to hate one another.

Chapter 23

New Olympus was as shiny as I remembered. The outer wall sparkled and made me think of diamonds. We strode across the bridge with our assortment of people trailing behind us. Some of the Valkyries that hadn't been enslaved had joined us on our journey.

No one attempted to stop us or interfere with us as we made our way to the throne room. Thor didn't wait to be announced. He simply shoved the door open and walked in. I was a few steps behind him, not entirely wanting to see the Greeks again, but knowing I would have to anyway.

We stopped once we reached the bottom of the dais that their thrones were placed on. I looked around, thinking they were even bigger than I remembered. I mentally shook myself from my stupor and squared my shoulders. I had to push the beginning inklings of fear back when my eyes landed on Hades.

"Thor, God of Thunder, what do we owe this displeasure?" Zeus asked, tapping his fingers on the arm of his chair. "When one wants to see the gods, one sends notice and asks for an appearance."

"Don't be condescending with me, Zeus." Thor's voice was laced with danger. "I sent word that I needed to speak with you about the treatment of my people, yet my letter has been ignored. When one doesn't respond, it makes the Norse gods annoyed, and we take action. We aren't the petty type that sleeps with our own family."

I felt myself blanche at this thought. I watched as Zeus's face turned an unpleasant shade of red. When his eyes met mine, I knew he recognized me. The red shade turned darker as his eyes narrowed, then he smiled.

"I see that you brought me a present, Thunderboy." Zeus gestured at me. "I've been looking for her. Almost had the twit until Loki and his whore thwarted me. Thank you for returning the vile creature."

Thunder echoed through the room, causing all the noise to stop. When the echoes of the thunder died down, Thor took two steps toward the god.

"You will not speak of my wife in such a manner. I shall skin you alive for any mistreatment of her." He spit out through gritted teeth. Then he turned to face Hades. "You and I also will have words about the treatment and imprisonment of my wife."

I touched his arm and gave it a reassuring squeeze. It wasn't the time to avenge my honor or whatever he planned. He met my eyes, and I shook my head no slightly. He took a deep breath and kissed my forehead before he turned his attention back to the hell-spawn in front of us.

"We shall discuss the treatment of Queen Kara another time. I am here now on behalf of my Valkyries. They are from Asgard and Valhalla, so they belong to me. You have wrongfully imprisoned and enslaved them. If you release them into my custody, I will forget that you have slighted me and mistreated the people of Asgard, henceforth Thunder Valley."

"And if I don't?" Zeus asked while examining his fingernails.

"Then I will destroy you and everyone you love."

"You can try, but you will not succeed. I will give you safe passage out of here if you leave now, but the woman stays. She has broken the law and must be punished."

"By Odin's beard, you will not lay a finger on the woman. She is mine, bound to me in the rights of our lands. She is the rightful queen of Thunder Valley and shall be treated as such."

Zeus rose and walked down the three steps of the dais to stand face to face with Thor. When he spoke, his voice was soft, yet deadly. "I will have what I want, you are no god. You are a boy with a hammer that is upset that someone took your playthings. I find it hilarious that your own uncle destroyed your home and killed so many, including the so-called mighty Odin. Now run along home with your toy hammer, and we will forget this day has happened."

His arm shot out quick as lightning, grabbing my arm and yanking me to him. I yelped out of surprise and pain as I was jerked from Thor's grip. I struggled against him, trying to free myself.

Zeus leaned forward, smelling my hair. "I see why you enjoy her so. I believe I will keep her as a plaything for a while. When I grow weary of her, I will do what I've wanted to do since I saw her, see her die. Hanging will be too quick. I'm sure Hades will give me some pointers on ways to dispose of her."

Thor lit up at that moment. It looked like lightning was coursing through his body and thunder was vibrating off him. I had never seen him look so frightening, yet majestic, as he looked at that moment.

His grip tightened on his hammer, and he raised his arm like he was going to start swinging.

"Stop!" a voice from the back of the room shouted.

Crimson made her way to the front of the room to stand between Thor and Zeus.

"No one moves a muscle. You have had ample time to see who had the bigger dick, now it's my turn to speak." She glanced back and forth at both men.

"What are you doing here?" Zeus asked, eyes narrowing at Crimson.

"You know why I'm here, Zeus. The same reason I've been here in the past and will continue to be here. I'm doing my job. You need to listen to me. I've been trying to get you to listen to me for the past three hundred years. You need to heed my warnings, or you will fall, again. Look how long it took you to rebuild from the last time. Now humans are scarce, and you are pitting yourself against those you will need in the coming times. Have I ever led you astray?"

"What do you want from me?" Zeus asked warily.

"Release the Valkyrie back into Thor's possession. If you refuse, you will be destroyed for all eternity."

"And release my people." Thor added.

Zeus shoved me back toward Thor; I stumbled, but he caught me and helped right me back on my feet. "There, you have the wench, now leave. I will not give you my slaves. They are mine. If you wanted them, you should have taken them to Thunder Valley with you, but no. You were too self-absorbed to do such a thing. You only cared about you. Those people came to me, and I gave them a place."

"You tortured them, made them less than nothing. How is that giving them a place?" I spat.

"Better than letting them wander around and die from the elements. Now leave."

"We will free my sisters. You will relinquish them to me." I demanded.

"You wish."

Zeus turned his back on us and left the room through a door that was behind the thrones. The other gods stood and followed suit.

Once alone, Thor led our people out of the palace. It wasn't until we were completely out of New Olympus that he spoke. He looked back at one of the guards that had been with us. "Go, send word to the others. We are going to free the Valkyries. I want the entire army here. Send for the other Valkyries as well, we will attack at dawn, so go in haste. Everyone else, make camp. The forest will provide adequate shelter."

He led me further into the forest, so we were completely by ourselves, before he turned to me and spoke. "You should have told me that your friend Crimson was an oracle."

I frowned. "I'm not sure what you mean. She isn't an oracle. She's Midgardian."

"My love, your friend is an oracle. She has been alive for centuries. You know that Midgardians don't survive more than a century. They age too fast. She spoke of things she has seen and warned Zeus of in the past. How do you know you can trust her?"

I thought about what he said. Things didn't seem to add up when it came to Crimson. Then her words from the cave came back into my mind. *That is my cross to bear at the moment.* I chewed on my lip as I thought about it.

"She nursed me back to health. She led us to you. Crimson has a true heart, I know it. If she were a warrior, I would be proud to bring her soul back to Valhalla. She has been nothing but loyal to me and she gave me her word that she wished to help. I trust her with my life, and it has been in her hands already since I met her."

"If you trust her that much, then I shall do my best to trust her as well, but I'll be keeping an eye on her." He leaned forward and placed a kiss on my lips. "Remember, I will do anything to ensure your safety. Now, let us make camp."

We built a small shelter to protect us from the elements where we were part of the crowd, yet separate enough that we had adequate privacy. Once camp was set up, we rejoined the others. I was surprised to see that more than our people were there.

One face I recognized immediately. Crispin, prince of the Seelie and Unseelie court. With him was a small army of his own. When we approached, he walked straight to us and bowed his head respectfully.

"Thor, God of Thunder, King of Thunder Valley, I am here to assist you in your endeavors of helping the Valkyries. I give you my armies of the Unseelie Court. It took some bribing, but I was granted permission to help. Lucian has also sent word that he will do what he can, but he's been stuck in Hourglass City for his part in freeing your wife."

He turned to me then and stepped forward. Instead of nodding like he did to Thor, he pulled me into his arms for a quick hug and kissed me lightly on the cheek. "Kara, it's good to see you well. I'm pleased to see that you made it to Thunder Valley and have reunited with your husband."

"Thank you for all you did. I apologize that Thor didn't believe you. I truly appreciate your help."

He smiled. "Don't thank me yet. Nothing is given freely. One day I may call upon you for help."

"I wouldn't expect anything less." I smiled. "Tis the warriors' way."

"Thank you, Crispin. I will appreciate all the help you are able to give. You have our allegiance. Now let's discuss strategy."

***

I awoke to Thor's arms wrapping around me. He had sent me to bed while he was planning with the promise that he would update me and everyone else in the morning. He had insisted that I needed rest, that my travels had been tiring, and I hadn't had much time to recover. I wasn't able to protest that.

My fingers found his arm and I slid them across his skin, effectively wrapping my arm around his neck. I could feel his breath gently caressing my skin. A shiver of excitement ran through me. It felt so incredibly right being in his arms.

I turned my head so that our lips were only a breath apart. His lips came down to mine and I couldn't suppress the moan that built up in my chest. I let it out gently into his mouth. His hand slid up from my waist to cup my breast. I arched my back to give him better access.

"I have dreamed of this for so long," he whispered as he trailed kisses from my lips to my neck. "I pictured our reunion being somewhere more comfortable than this, yet I can't think of anywhere else I'd want to be right now."

I turned in his arms so that I was facing him. "I love you. I've missed you so. When we were apart, it

185

felt as if my heart was missing. You complete me, my husband."

"You are my all, I will enjoy showing you how much I missed you."

I could feel the evidence of how much he missed me pressing into my belly. It sent sensations through me that I had never felt before. I kissed him, following my instincts. My legs seemed to wrap around him on their own accord.

"Ahem." A sound from behind me made me freeze.

"You better have a bloody good reason to be interrupting the reunion with my wife, or I will peel the skin off your body with my bare hands." Thor growled.

"I beg forgiveness, my lord, but you wished that I let you know when the troops arrived. The sun will be up in a matter of hours and the first of the army has arrived. Along with the rest of Prince Crispin's people."

"Fine. I'll be there in a moment. Thank you, Raven." Footsteps receding announced that we were once again alone.

I felt the burn of embarrassment on my cheeks. I had been caught in a precarious position with Thor. Then I reminded myself that he was my husband and being in his arms was something that would be expected of a wife. I wasn't truly certain how to be a wife.

Thor kissed me again, erasing my brain from any thoughts. "We must rise and free our people. When we have succeeded and are back home, you and I will retire to our chambers where I will show you how much I love you. There will be no interruptions and we will work on making children."

I untangled myself from him. He stood, holding a hand out to me. I took it and rose from the ground. We had a battle to wage and there wasn't time for romance.

CHAPTER 24

T he army was much larger than I had imagined it would be. I stared at the sea of warriors and my heart swelled with pride. All of this to free my sisters, the other Valkyries. It was an overwhelming, humbling feeling.

What surprised me the most was when Brynhild limped up through the lines to me. She knelt before me, placing a hand on her heart, lowering her head.

"Kara, I must apologize to you for the way I treated you before. You have shown the strength and greatness that is important in being a leader. You have shown that they were correct about your potential. I am proud to serve you. My queen." She spoke softly, but the words carried.

One by one, the other Valkyries followed suit and knelt before me, giving me their allegiance. "Please rise. I am honored you think so highly of me, yet I've done nothing that you wouldn't do. Let's get our sisters back. We will fight 'til our deaths if need be."

Thor gave the word and the army started to march to New Olympus. He put his arm around me and tightened his grip. He spun Mjolnir in circles to gain speed, then thrust his arm in the air. We shot up into the sky and took flight above the army. When we dropped to the ground again, we were standing at the gate of New Olympus.

"Zeus, this is your last chance. Release the Valkyries or face the battle ahead. I will not show you mercy if you refuse to surrender the Valkyries to me." Thor's voice thundered through the air.

A laugh echoed around us. "Oh, child, you are quite amusing. Your little army doesn't stand a chance against what we have. We will crush you into dust."

"We may not have the numbers, but we have something you don't. Fortitude. We want our warriors back. The Valkyries are much more than slaves, they are women of great power and skill. They are to be revered and treated with respect. We will have them back, no matter the cost." He gave the signal and the army rushed forward.

I swung my sword with all my might and felt it bite into the closest of the Greek's warriors. A primal joy of the kill surged through me. I hadn't felt that in a long time. I didn't take pleasure in killing and would never do so just for pleasure, but on an animal level, it was satisfying. I knew that every strike of my sword got me that much closer to my sisters' freedom.

A wave of warriors from behind us flooded the area and I could hear the cries of injury and death. After this battle, I was certain there would be several warrior souls ready to go to Valhalla. The thought made me pause. Valhalla was no more. The thought of my home being gone made my heart ache. I briefly wondered what would happen to all the warriors' souls. Taking a deep breath, I pushed those thoughts out of my mind. I couldn't afford the distraction at the moment.

As our troops pushed deeper into New Olympus, I looked for Thor through the throngs of people. I knew he was doing what he did best, but that didn't mean I still didn't worry about him. I knew that he was a great warrior, but I couldn't help myself. My love for him made me worry. After spotting him, a tightness in my chest loosened. If all went well, we would both survive this fight.

Minutes turned into hours as the battle drew on. My arms and shoulders burned from swinging the sword like I had been. If I was so sore, I could only imagine how the others were feeling. This was what I had been born to do. What I was trained for. Others who were standing at our side weren't trained for the grueling hell of war. More would start to fall as they tired. It was inevitable.

Trumpets sounded in the distance, causing me to pause out of surprise. I knew better than to let myself become distracted in war; it could be a fatal mistake, but the sound had been unexpected. All I had heard for hours was the sound of fighting and death. The blow caught me off guard and I hit the ground with a resounding thud. Pain shot up my spine and, looking up at the soldier that stood over me, I knew my end was near. The distraction had proven to be fatal.

As the soldier's blade came swinging down at me, I refused to flinch or look away. There was nothing I could do to prevent it, but I knew I could control how I died. The blade came mere inches from my face when the soldier's back arched and he froze. His eyes widened in shock. The tip of a blade protruded from his chest, blood dripping from it. He was yanked out of my line of sight and a shadow replaced him.

I blinked several times before the shadow moved so I had a better view of the person looming over me. It was Mist. She held a hand out for me. I put my hand in hers and she pulled me to my feet.

"I couldn't let you have all the fun, sister." she said as she steadied me on my feet. "When I heard the that the warriors from Thunder Valley were storming New Olympus, I knew I had to come. Our sisters will finally get the freedom they deserve. Let us do this and bring our sisters home. Loki is here as well as his army. We couldn't let you go it alone."

I looked past her shoulder to see that what she said was true. An army was coming out of the trees at a run and were joining the fighting. If I didn't know better, it appeared as if the new warriors relished the fight that they were joining.

My eyes met Mist's. A small smile formed at the corners of my mouth. "Thank you, sister. I knew that you weren't a betrayer. Let's do this."

We turned at the same time, jumping back into the fight. Having Mist join me in the battle seemed to rejuvenate my determination to free the others. We moved together, mirroring the other's movements as we had a thousand times during our practices and training.

As I crossed the threshold of the gates to New Olympus, the sky began to cloud over, and a storm rolled in. The smell of rain flooded my senses as the first drops splattered on the ground. Then it was as if a dam burst, and sheets of rain fell from the sky. I was drenched in seconds. The ground beneath me turned to mud, causing my feet to slide slightly from lack of traction.

The further I made my way into New Olympus, the harder the rain fell. I could barely see with the water in my eyes and the turrets falling around me. I knew that I had to make my way to the palace if I were going to have a chance to save my sisters.

A scream ripped through me as an arrow pierced my right shoulder. The sword fell from my hand as a tingling shot down my arm from the wound. My knees buckled and I struggled to keep my feet. I looked at the arrow protruding from my shoulder. I was going to have to remove it if I was going to keep fighting.

I held my breath and gripped the shaft of the arrow. I was about to pull it out when Thor appeared out of nowhere in front of me. His hand covered mine, stopping me from removing it.

"Wait," he said softly as he looked at the arrow. "You will cause more damage to your shoulder if you pull it back out. I will help you with it. I'm sorry, my love, but it will hurt. A lot."

He moved behind me and I felt him grab the arrowhead. There was a loud snap before he came back around and ripped the shaft from my arm. The tip was missing from the arrow when it came free from my shoulder, so I assumed he broke off the tip before removing it.

His hands cupped my face and his mouth met mine briefly. "There. Now go show them what you are made of, my queen. It's time we end this."

I couldn't have agreed with him more. I reached down, picking up my sword even though the pain in my shoulder was enough that I wanted to scream again. I refused to show anymore the weakness from the pain. Once was all they were going to get from me. I rolled my shoulder a few times, trying to get the feeling back in my hand. I wasn't sure I would be able to fight with that hand if the feeling didn't come back into it. Since the tingling didn't let up, I switched my sword to my left hand. I wasn't as strong of a fighter with my left, but I would make do.

As we fought our way to the palace doors, there were less soldiers to get through and the rain lessened. I looked at Thor, wondering if he noticed that as well. He gave a half shrug as he ripped the head off a soldier and tossed it to the ground without hesitation.

We stepped up to the doors. Before we could try them, they flew open as if a force kicked them in. I glanced at Thor again as I stepped across the threshold. I knew we were walking into a trap, but every fiber in my being told me there really wasn't a choice if I wanted to end this war and free the Valkyries.

Chapter 25

The Great Hall was empty when we reached it. As I looked around the hall, seeing no one or anything in the room, the muscles in my shoulders began to tense. Something was greatly wrong. The dais that once had contained the seats of the gods and the golden throne was empty.

"Thor, this room had thrones in it when we were here last." My mind whirled with possibilities. Had it all been an illusion before? I was certain it hadn't been, but I had been preoccupied with the treatment of my people then.

"Yes, it did. From what I know of the Greeks, which honestly isn't much, they are big on self-preservation and tend to be cowardly. Where we fight for our people, they send their people to fight for them." He turned, looking around the room as well. "Come. We will find them. I know Zeus is here. I can feel his presence."

"What do you mean, feel his presence?" I cocked an eyebrow but didn't look at him. I was still picturing the room as it had been before.

"We have similar abilities, so it is almost a calling of power. That is the best way I can describe it."

"Then let's find him."

Without any more discussion, we started searching the palace for Zeus and the others. I knew that Thor was correct. They had to be there somewhere. There weren't many places they could hide. After spending what seemed like hours searching the palace, we made our way back to the grand hall.

The anxiety and readiness of the battle made me itchy, and I wanted to get to it. I could still hear the sounds of battle coming from the windows, so I knew the war raged on outside still. If Zeus didn't show himself soon, I would rather be out there with the others fighting.

I approached the dais where I would have a better view of the battles ensuing outside in the rain and elements. I could see the slain littering the ground. The dead were from both sides. It had to end soon or there would be none left to fight.

I felt a breeze on the back of my neck. My hand went to it automatically to block the cool air. There hadn't been a breeze where Thor still stood. Why was I feeling one all of a sudden? I turned to study the room. The only windows were where I had been looking out, so there was nowhere else for the air to come from unless . . .

"There's a hidden passage in here," I said abruptly.

Thor's eyes shot to mine. "What?"

"There is a passage in here somewhere. I don't know where, but I know there is one. There has to be. Like you said, they wouldn't go far, and you can still feel Zeus's presence. That means there has to be another exit from this room."

I stalked around the room, looking for any telltale signs that there was a passage. I circled the room three times, not seeing any clues that there was a passageway. Doubts crept into my mind. Maybe I had imagined the breeze and there really weren't any passages and the Greeks had beaten us. The last thought stopped me in my tracks. I couldn't let my mind and doubts take over.

Taking a deep breath, I closed my eyes and let my instincts take over. There was something else that seemed to grip me when I exhaled the second time. It was a tightening in my chest, making breathing difficult. My heart began to race in excitement. I felt like something was starting to tug at me. I wanted to follow it.

My eyes shot open, and I turned toward the wall behind the dais. It was in that direction that the invisible tug had been pulling at me. The sensation was still there, and I couldn't help myself but abide by that sensation. Following the tugging, I approached the wall.

I examined the wall before me. It would have seemed like an ordinary wall, except it was the only one that had any adornment. It was a painting of Zeus in his glory. It was almost like there was a beacon signaling its location. It had to be there. I ran over and began to run my hands over it, trying to find the latch.

My hand ran over a bump in the groin of the painting of Zeus and I couldn't help but roll my eyes. The ego of the gods. I pushed in and there was a loud click. The wall popped slightly ajar.

"This way," I whispered. I didn't know why, but I knew that I needed to keep my voice low. I didn't want to be heard.

I slipped into the darkness of the passageway and could feel the cool breeze again. Then there was a warmth on my back that comforted me because I knew it was Thor. We navigated the long passage that seemed to twist and turn like a maze. Suddenly it went upward, and it felt like we were climbing up the side of a mountain.

When it leveled out, I glanced back at Thor to see that his muscles were bunched. He had to be feeling like I was. I was ready to fight. I knew Thor had a taste for battle, so he was dying for the fight.

As soon as the word dying flashed through my mind, I pictured him lying prone on the ground like all the other warriors we had lost during the battle. It caused my heart to constrict, and I had to remind myself that he wasn't dead. He was alive and well right behind me.

We entered a large, cavernous room that was lit only by torches. The room reminded me of my time spent in Hourglass City. It had been dark with torches lighting the way there as well. I had to suppress a shudder as the memories flooded me. I wasn't still there.

My mind was brought back to the present when I heard a sinuous laugh echo through the room. My eyes settled on Hades, who was standing next to Zeus.

"Well, well, well." Hades's lips curled in a bone-chilling smile. "Look what the cat dragged in. I'm surprised such a little imp was able to find us."

"You would be quite surprised by what I can do," I retorted. I could feel Thor step closer to me. I wasn't sure if it was a protective move or if he was ready to spring into action. "Stop the fighting and release my people. If you don't, more people will die for a war that could have been prevented."

"If I released my slaves, then who would serve me?" Zeus asked, quirking his lips.

"That is not my problem. I command you, release my people."

"I think not." Zeus laughed and waved a hand at me.

"Release our people," Thor's voice boomed through the room, making it feel smaller than it was. "Zeus, I grow wary of your tomfoolery. You only prolong this to irritate my wife. My patience is at its end."

"My tomfoolery? Who do you think you are, *boy*?" Zeus stressed the word boy. "You were a twinkle in your father's eye when I took power. You have nothing on me. I will do as I please. Now take your splittail and go before I grow tired of your presence."

Thor charged Zeus at the insult to me, his hammer swinging as he neared him. "I will smash your skull for speaking of my wife in such an ill manner!"

When Zeus and Thor collided, the room erupted in chaos. Lightning lit the room in flashes that made everything look as if it were moving in slow motion. The Valkyries that were being chained and manacled were starting to fight the guards.

The other gods, aside from Hades, disappeared from the room. Hades leaned against the wall, watching the fighting with what could only be called amusement on his face. I made my way across the room so that we were face to face. I drew my sword and pointed it at him.

"We have some business to finish." I told him grimly.

He chuckled. "Do we now?"

"Aye. Before it is done, you will be impaled by my sword." I pointed my sword at him.

He didn't seem perturbed by that; he simply crossed his arms over his chest. He looked almost relaxed. When I was close enough to stab him with my sword, he just back handed me, knocking the sword out of my hand. I was sent backward. I landed hard enough on my butt to make my teeth snap together.

The impact of Mjolnir hitting the ground shook the room. I turned in time to see a snake latching onto Thor's neck as he fell backwards, trying to get the snake to release its grip from him. I sprang toward him, pulling a dagger from my boot.

In one swift arc of the dagger, I cut the head off the serpent then pried its head off Thor's neck. He stopped moving and his eyes rolled back in his head. I wasn't sure, but I thought the snake had been poisonous. I didn't get a good enough look at its eyes, but I didn't imagine the Greeks would keep a harmless snake on them to attack Thor with.

"Thor, wake up," I shook his shoulders, trying to rouse him. "Please, you have to wake up."

A shadow loomed over me as my attention had been focused solely on Thor. I looked up to see Zeus staring down at me, smiling. He had a lightning bolt in his hand, and he looked positively evil from where I knelt.

"Now, little imp, all I have to do is take care of you and I can put an end to this ridiculousness." He held the lightning bolt up like he was going to throw it at me. I stared him down, trying to weigh my options.

A cry of rage came from behind me and before the bolt could hit me, someone jumped in the way, taking the full force of the lightning bolt into them. The body hit the ground in front of us with a resounding thud.

Surprise and horror swept through me as I saw Brynhild lying on the ground. Her skin was burned and blackened, and smoke rose from her body. The smell of burned flesh was acrid. It smelled like a boar that had been over cooked to the point of charcoal. Her chest heaved unsteadily.

I scrambled to her to cradle her head in my lap. Tears gathered behind my eyes and a lump formed in my throat. "Brynhild. No. Why did you do that?"

Brynhild coughed, expelling blood from her mouth. "Kara, it was—my destiny to save you. Your mother. Your mother would be so proud of you. She told me that you would do great things. I wish I would have believed that. Do what you need to in order to save us. It's your destiny. You are a queen now. A goddess. Give them—" She was cut off with a coughing fit. She smiled at me, teeth covered in blood. "Hell."

Her eyes rolled up and her chest stopped rising and falling. Tears dripped off my face, landing on hers with soft plops. I gently wiped the tears from her face and looked up at Zeus with all the rage that I felt. I carefully moved Brynhild's head off my lap and rose, not knowing what I was going to do. I just let the feelings take over me.

The rage was a warmth that made my blood, which had been running cold, boil. I was tired of being treated like a nothing. Anger for the way my sisters were being held captive burned inside me like nothing I had ever felt. I held a hand up to Zeus and he flew backward, slamming into the wall.

Out of the corner of my eye, I saw Hades taking a step toward me and I did the same to him. He hit the wall as well. I could see them struggling, but neither could get free. I walked closer to Zeus until we were face to face.

"You *will* free my sisters, all of the Valkyries." I commanded. My voice seemed to echo through the room. I could see that the fighting had stopped, and everyone stared in my direction. "I command it, so mote it be."

"What- what if I don't?" Zeus rasped out.

I stepped so close to him that my nose was almost touching him. I dropped my voice so it was barely audible, "If you don't, then I will rip you apart, limb from limb. I will start by cutting off your manhood so you can't make any more bastards. Once you are in pieces, I will cut off your head and feed it to the hellhounds."

When Zeus didn't concede, I held my hand out, my dagger flying from the ground where it had been dropped and landing in my hand. Without breaking eye contact with him, I took my other hand and began to feel around his robes for his manhood. When I found it, I squeezed it and took my dagger, placing it against his groin. I pressed the edge of the blade against him. He yelped and began to struggle.

"Fine," he ground out.

"Pardon?" I asked sweetly. "I don't think I heard you and I'm not sure what you meant."

"Release the servants," he commanded quickly. His eyes met mine. There was a fire in them that normally would have made my skin crawl. "Now release me."

"Hmm," I pondered and smiled at him. "Now you are making demands of me? You are lucky that I'm not going to kill you where you stand."

"You can't kill me," he spat. "I'm immortal, you fool."

"True," I shrugged. "That doesn't mean that I couldn't chop you into pieces so you would have to spend eternity scattered across Midgard."

Once the room was empty of Valkyries, I stepped back and released Zeus and Hades from the hold I had them in. I turned and made my way back to Thor, noticing that he still hadn't moved since he had been bitten by the snake.

I knelt beside him, placing my hands over the bite. I wondered if there was anything I could do to help him, but I didn't think so. Tears welled in my eyes. He didn't appear to be breathing. Leaning down, I pressed my lips to his mouth.

"Please wake up," I whispered to him. "I just found you again and can't live without you."

I pushed a hand to his chest and felt the slight flutter of his heart. I needed to get him to the healers immediately. I looked up at Zeus once more, anger burning in my gut.

"If he doesn't live, I will be back and I *will* find a way to kill you. No god is completely immortal. I just have to find your weakness. Believe me when I tell you that I will. I won't stop until I find a way to destroy you."

With those words, I looked back down at Thor and thought of home. Asgard. My heart skipped a beat and broke a little more when I realized we couldn't go back there. Then I thought of the home he made. Thunder Valley. The room began to spin and suddenly we were no longer in the room with the Greeks.

Chapter 26

I looked around to see that we were now on the floor of the Great Hall in Thunder Valley. Confused and slightly nauseated, I stared at the wall, trying to regain my bearings. When it finally sank in that we were temporarily safe, I turned my attention back to Thor.

He still hadn't moved or roused. I leaned over him, the side of my face closer to his mouth. I could feel the soft tufts of air coming from his mouth as he breathed. It was faint, but still there. Relieved, I leaned back. As long as he was breathing, I had a little bit of time to fix him.

The relief was short lived, however, when I got a good look at the wound. There were black streaks running from the bite up his neck. It also streaked down under his armor. Gently, I lifted him up and removed the chest plate with shaking hands. The black streaks ran down his chest and stopped above his heart.

I didn't know anything about snakes, but I knew that the streaks were a bad sign. If the poison reached his heart, it would kill him. I sat back on my haunches, unable to take my eyes off him. I was going to lose him after just being reunited with him again. My heart broke as my mind raced, trying to come up with a way to save him. Tears gathered behind my eyes and a lump formed at the back of my throat. The thought of losing him was more than I could bear.

"What is this?" a voice asked from the doorway.

I turned to see an elderly woman wearing an apron over her skirts standing there. Her skirts were a deep blue with a trim of white. She was wringing her hands in her apron as she stared at us.

"Is that my lord?" She rushed over and knelt on the other side of him. "Oh my! Ingrid, get the apothecary quickly! The king is injured. Send for some men to help get him to his chambers."

The other woman, Ingrid, whom I hadn't seen in the room before, darted out and I could hear her footsteps running down the hall.

"I can move him," I insisted.

"No, Miss." Her voice was tight as she pressed a hand to Thor's shoulder to keep him in place. "I can't let you move him. If you jostle him too much, the poison will spread. We will get the men to carry him. They know what they are doing when it comes to moving people."

"Who are you?" I asked, a frown forming on my face.

"My dear, Kara, I am Sjofn." She smiled at me. The smile was kind, warm, and full of love. "I've been watching over Thor since we came to this dreadful place and made it our home."

Before anything else could be said, the room filled with men and chaos. We were pushed away from Thor, and he was surrounded by guards who moved in sync to lift and carry him. The movement was fluid like he weighed nothing at all. As they carried him from the room, they moved slowly so as not to jostle him. The progress was almost painful to watch. I wanted to hurry them so we could get him taken care of.

The procession leading up to his bed chambers left a silence in its wake. The servants and others that we passed on our way stopped what they were doing to stare. All talking ceased. By the time we made it to Thor's chambers, the silence in the castle was deafening.

Sjofn opened the door to his chamber and held the door for the men to pass through. Once inside, they gently placed him on the bed and stepped back. I rushed forward, pushing my way through. The streaks had spread up the side of his face and a darkness started to stain his chest.

"Where's the apothecary?" I demanded.

"He will be here soon," Sjofn promised. "We just have to be patient."

"We don't have time to be patient. He's dying."

"Aye, he is, but rushing things won't make him heal. The apothecary has to bring the correct elixir, or it will cause more damage than it will help."

"If he doesn't show up soon, then Thor will die from the poison." My voice sounded shrill, even to my own ears.

Sjofn moved from her position opposite me, walking around the bed so she was standing beside me. Her hand went to my shoulder, squeezing it lightly. Then she turned me so I was facing her. When my eyes stayed on Thor, she took my chin and turned my head until I was looking at her.

"Listen, child, I've been around for longer than you can imagine. I have seen death many times over and have watched Thor grow from a wee babe. I have seen him defeat death before, or his soul would have been in Valhalla long before now. You need to trust me." Sjofn's voice was soothing and felt like it was trying to lull me into complacency.

I stiffened and jerked away from her even though my body wanted to relax and let her take all the stress into herself. I couldn't do that. Thor was mine and I wouldn't place that burden on anyone else aside from me.

The door swung open and a tall, skinny man with a long, white beard came rushing into the room. His arms were loaded down with different sized vials. He was followed by a young woman in a white dress carrying a bowl of water and a towel, and a woman in grey carrying bandages.

All the supplies were set on the table next to the bed. Once everything was set up in an order I didn't understand, the apothecary turned and addressed the room. "I want everyone out. I need to concentrate."

After the room emptied out, the man turned and glared at me. "I said everyone out."

I crossed my arms over my chest and leveled a glare at him. "No."

"Don't make me force you out."

"I'd like to see you try. You touch me, old man, and I'll rip you apart, limb from limb, with my bare hands."

"Merlin," Sjofn interjected, "this is his majesty's wife, Kara."

His eyebrows shot up as he stared at me. "You are the missing wife? The Valkyrie?"

I didn't answer, just motioned toward Thor. My jaw was clenched so tight that it was starting to ache. "Fix him now."

Merlin nodded once and turned his attention away from me to Thor. He leaned over and sniffed the bite mark on Thor's neck. Then he inhaled deeply. "You should have called for me sooner."

"I called you as soon as they appeared in the Great Hall." Sjofn turned to me. "How long ago was he bitten?"

Panic raced through my veins, tightening my chest. It felt like someone was grabbing my heart and squeezing it as hard as they could. I thought my heart was going to burst. It began to pound harder like it was trying to free itself from the grip on it. My mind raced, trying to remember when during the fighting it had happened. I shook my head slightly. "I don't remember. We were battling."

Disappointment flooded the room, making me feel like I was going to drown in it. Sjofn placed her hand on my shoulder once again and gave it a reassuring squeeze. "It's alright, my child. I understand time goes differently in battle. We will heal him."

"That's easy for you to say," grumbled Merlin as he washed the wound with the water from the bowl. "The poison has spread far into his body. I can smell the decay from it killing the body."

He reached for vials and began pouring them into Thor's mouth, manipulating his neck to make him swallow. Then Merlin leaned over and listened for Thor's breath again. Grumbling to himself, he poured a different vial of liquid down his throat.

"It isn't working. Why isn't it working?" I hadn't realized I had said it aloud until I got a sharp look from Merlin.

"You waited too long to get him assistance."

I took a step forward, my arm shooting out to grab the old man by the neck. "I got him here as soon as I could. You are the one who took their sweet time getting up here with your witchcraft. Now you fix him, or your head will be on the chopping block."

Merlin's eyes widened as they bulged from the pressure I was putting on his neck. His mouth opened and closed but no words came out. There were a few choking sounds, but that was it.

"Kara!" Sjofn scolded. "Release him and let him work. It is neither of your fault that he is in the situation that he is in. We all know that Thor goes into battle headlong without a thought to the consequences and we do not expect anything different."

I released my grip and strode to the window to look out. In the distance, I could see the troops arriving from the battle. Many were injured and being carried by those less injured. Guilt swamped me when I realized that I had left them alone to fight themselves when Thor had been injured. And I had left Brynhild's soul and body at New Olympus. She deserved to come home.

Home. The thought was another blow to my system. We didn't have a home. A place for the Valkyries and the souls of the warriors to go. The thought had crossed my mind once before during the battle, but I hadn't had time to truly think about it until just then.

Sjofn came to stand beside me. I didn't look at her, but I could feel her standing there. She didn't say anything for several minutes. When she spoke, her voice was soft and careful. "Merlin has done all he can. Thor is resting, but I don't think he has much longer to live. Let us treat your shoulder, then we will leave the two of you alone so you can say your farewells."

I touched the shoulder I had forgotten about. It hadn't hurt with all the excitement, now it burned.

When I pulled my hand away, there was blood on my fingertips. Slowly, I shook my head no. "My shoulder will heal in due time. Leave it be. Leave us. I don't deserve to be healed with magicks. It will heal on its own."

I turned and faced the man who had fought to save Thor. I studied him and could see the weariness and sadness etched into his face. I knew then that he had done everything he could to save my husband.

"You did your best. Now it is time for me to spend some time alone with him. Sjofn is correct. It is time to say goodbye. I will let you know when it is done."

With that, I watched them gather their things and quietly slip out of the room. I looked back to the bed where Thor was lying prone. My heart shattered as I approached him. As carefully as I could, I joined him on the bed. I sat next to him without touching him. I was afraid to touch him. His breathing was shallow and erratic.

"I should be angry with you," I said to him softly. "In fact, I am very angry with you. You promised we would be together. I'm angry that you broke that promise. I hurt. When we came through the Bi-Frost and were separated, I thought I could live with the fact we weren't meant to be together longer than we were. I was accepting of that. I went through hell and found my way back to you. I thought then that we would finally have our forever. Now you aren't letting that happen. You gave up."

I stood up and paced the room. "You let a snake best you! A snake. I know the prophecy was a serpent, but it was supposed to be Jörmungandr, not a small snake. I'm angry you were that weak. You gave up on me, on us. You mustn't have thought that we would win the fight, so you quit. I never knew you were a quitter, but you showed me that you were. Now you are done fighting."

Spinning, I turned and faced the bed and Thor once again. "What will happen to your soul? You don't have Valhalla to go to. Maybe you will go to Helheim. Or the place Hades calls Hourglass City. Is that what you deserve? A warrior doesn't give up."

I dropped to my knees as the pain crushed me. The tears that I had been fighting back began to fill my eyes and spill over. "I'm mad at myself. I shouldn't have let you go with me. It wasn't your battle, it was mine. I'm angry that I was selfish. When I saw you collapse, you were all I could think of. Love made me weak. It was supposed to make me stronger, but it didn't. I don't want to live without you. Please don't leave me. I don't belong on Midgard or any of the realms or worlds without you, my love. I'm angry at myself for not being strong enough to let you go. Please don't go. I love you."

I stayed on my knees by the bed as I watched the last breath escape him. He went still and the room fell silent except for the sound of my sniffles as the tears fully escaped and I started to cry, mourning the loss of my soulmate.

Chapter 27

O nce I was spent of tears, I uncurled from the ball I made on the floor. My legs hurt, so did my head, eyes, throat, and chest. I sniffled and wiped at my eyes, trying to dry them. My eyes went to Thor's lifeless form on the bed, and I felt my breath catch.

I inched closer and climbed onto the bed next to him. Gently, I brushed his hair from his face. His skin was still warm to the touch, so he hadn't been gone for long. Leaning over, I placed a kiss on his cooling lips. I couldn't bring myself to say goodbye to him quite yet.

We hadn't had enough time. I didn't think there would ever be enough time. Yet he was taken from me too soon. I didn't know what to do. I missed him dreadfully. I was still angry with him, but I was just as angry with myself. I was being weak. Valkyries weren't weak.

I had to get myself right but couldn't seem to figure out how. I decided to give myself a few more minutes alone, to grieve before I had to stuff my feelings back inside and bury them deep. I stared down at his peaceful face, thinking about what could have been even though it wouldn't do any good.

The door of the bed chamber opened, and I glared at it as I waited for the being to come into view.

Crimson's head appeared around the edge of the door, and she made eye contact with me.

"Is everything alright, Kara?" Her voice was soft and filled with concern. It made my chest constrict.

I shook my head no and looked away so she couldn't see the tears gathering once more. "Leave us. I will find you when we are done here."

"I'll be waiting." With that, the door shut quietly behind her.

Once we were alone again, I rested my head beside his and closed my eyes, thinking about our wedding day. *Thor took me by the waist and danced around the floor with me. Instead of music playing, he hummed a melody in my ear. I was floating across the floor with him. It was a tune of our people to celebrate a union of souls.*

I hadn't been happier than when Thor made me his wife. Our happiness had been short lived then too. Perhaps we weren't meant to be together. Our hearts were meant to be broken. Yet, that dance after our nuptials was forever burned into my mind and heart. It had been full of promise that we were going to be together.

"We never got to celebrate our union. Now we have to honor your passing," I whispered into his ear. "I'm not sure I can bear it. I don't know how to tell the people of Thunder Valley we lost our king and valiant warrior. To a snake, no less. But for a little bit, it will be my grief and my secret."

I rose again and went to the window to look out. I could hear music playing. It was a joyous sound in celebration of the freeing of the Valkyries. It wasn't fair to them to ruin the celebration, so I decided to give them the evening to feel the joy and triumph.

I pulled the curtains closed, enveloping us in darkness. I didn't light a candle or start a fire. In the dark, I could pretend that he was still with me. I went back to the bed and took his stiff cooling hand in mine. I sat there, staring at the wall and holding his hand. I wasn't aware of how the time passed. I could have sat there for minutes, hours, or days, yet I had no idea.

When I finally decided it was time to let them all know, I climbed off the bed and my joints were stiff and sore from sitting for so long. I went out the door into the hallway. Crimson and Sjofn were both sitting outside the door. Crimson was knitting and Sjofn was just staring at the wall.

"What are you doing?" I asked incredulously.

"Waiting for you," Crimson replied as she set whatever it was she was knitting onto her lap and looked up at me. "How are you doing?"

I shook my head, not wanting to discuss me. I addressed Sjofn instead. "I need you to assemble everyone in the kingdom. Place black flags up. We will mourn our king properly. Have the men build a funeral pyre so we can give Thor a proper send off."

"Are we going to send him out to sea?" Sjofn asked.

I shook my head no. "Thor wouldn't want that."

She gave me a nod and rose off the floor. Once she disappeared down the hallway, I turned my attention to Crimson.

"I thought you would return to your hut after the final battle."

"That is one of the items I wished to speak to you about. I was told that my village and my hut no longer remain. They were destroyed during the battle. Also, Zeus knows that I helped you, so I'll be a target when

I return." She stood as she spoke, so she was eye level with me.

"Then you will stay here with me." I declared.

"I've been provided a cottage outside the walls that I'd be more than happy to stay at."

"Crimson," I took her hands and looked her in the eyes. "When Zeus realizes that you stayed here, you wouldn't be safe outside of the walls. You will live inside the walls. The palace is large enough, you can have your own wing if you wish for distance and privacy."

"That isn't necessary, my queen. It is appreciated, but I only need a room. I will help around the palace."

"Nonsense. You are a dear friend and trusted advisor to the queen. You will not need to lift a finger for the rest of your days. I insist." I leaned over and kissed her cheek. "I will need you when I let the people know of Thor's passing. I'm not sure I have the strength to do this."

"You are much stronger than you think, my dear." Crimson squeezed my hands in comfort. "Come. Let's get you something to eat and drink. You must be ravenous. You have been in the room with him for two days' time."

"Two days?" The amount of time amazed me because he still hadn't been cold to the touch. Yes, his body temperature had dropped immensely, but he wasn't as cold as I thought he would be for being dead.

"Yes, two days. You need to eat."

"I can't. Not until this is done. Let's go to the Great Hall. I will inform the people there."

***

The Great Hall was so filled with people, it was standing room only. I stood on the riser that Thor used

214

for his throne, Crimson standing behind me in case I needed her. There were rumblings and whispers about the noticeable absence of the God of Thunder and ruler of Thunder Valley.

"Attention!" My voice echoed through the room as it fell silent. Thunder rolled outside as if the sky knew what I was about to say. "I regret that I have to inform you about the death of Thor."

The rumble of chatter raced through the room, making my ears ring. There were exclamations of disbelief and denials. I heard at least one person accuse me of lying.

"I know this is hard to believe, and he will be greatly missed. Our great king fell in battle. He died doing what he loved the most. Fighting, killing. Everything to save him was done, it didn't work. Tomorrow at sunset, we will set him upon the pyre, and we will see him off."

With that, I left the room in a hustle. I wasn't in the mood to hear what others had to say about the death of the love of my life. Once alone with Crimson, I dropped to the floor, breathing hard. I pressed one fist to my stomach and the other to my chest. I was having trouble catching my breath and controlling my emotions.

The thunder crashed outside, and rain began to splatter against the roof as the storm inside me waged. Crimson sat on the floor next to me, wrapping her arms around me in an embrace that was meant to either restrain or comfort, I wasn't sure which.

We sat there in silence, except for my sobs, while the storm raged on outside. Once I quieted down, Crimson released me. She stood and went to the table to pour a cup of tea. She returned with it and sat back down.

"Here, this will soothe and numb the pain, just for a little while. I know what you did was impossibly hard, but you did well. Not many widows could stand and tell a room full of people that their king, her husband, was dead without losing composure. You did well this evening. Now you need to rest because tomorrow will be more difficult. You will need to pick out what you want him to wear as his last outfit and prepare for the wake and meal afterwards. I will be with you every step of the way, but it won't be easy. Nothing with this will be easy, so please, Kara, take tonight."

I nodded. She was right and I knew it. I had a lot to do the next day and I was going to have to be strong. Even after the funeral, I was going to have to stay strong for the kingdom. I had big shoes to fill, and I was nowhere near ready to be the queen, not without my king. I never wanted to be a queen.

With shaking hands, I took the teacup from her hands and slowly sipped. Not only did it soothe me, I became incredibly tired and had to fight to keep my eyes open. I knew I was losing the fight when everything went blurry.

Before I fell into oblivion, I heard Crimson whisper, "I am here, my queen. Just rest now and we will deal with everything in the morn."

Sleep pulled me under so quickly, I didn't have a chance to be angry with her for drugging me.

Chapter 28

The storm rolled on through the day. The rain came down so hard that it sounded like drums pounding on the windows. It was almost like the weather was matching my mood. There was darkness in my heart and soul as the time to place Thor on the pyre drew nearer.

I walked into his room—I had refused to have him moved since he passed—and approached his bedside. Smiling down at him, my heart, which had been precariously held together, shattered. I knew that I would love him for the rest of my days even though he was no longer with me. Leaning over, I kissed his cool forehead and turned away. It was time to get him ready for the ceremony.

I strode to the closet and pulled it open. I studied the clothing he had in there and couldn't help but smile. He was a man of simple pleasures. There were tunics, all the same color. Black. He didn't have anything that was worthy of a king and great warrior's pyre. As I prepared to call the tailor, I stopped myself. He wouldn't want to be known as anything but what he was. Thor, the man.

"Kara, there are people to do this for you. You don't have to do it on your own. You should focus on yourself and how you are going to deal with the ceremony." Crimson stood in the doorway, her hand on the door. "This is going to be harder than you think."

"Crimson, I have to do it. I have to be doing something. If I don't, then I'm going to break. I've sent the messengers and a team back to New Olympus to retrieve our fallen. They deserve to come home and be honored. We will honor them tonight as well, and deal with their bodies when they return. I have the archers ready and in place for the ceremony. But I can't stop. I just can't. I have to get through the day." I turned my back to her, and my eyes landed on Thor again. That ache made it hard to breathe. When I spoke again, my voice was barely a whisper. "I don't know how to go on once it's done. He's gone. He's what kept me going all these years."

"Let me help you. He needs a fresh tunic. We should make sure he is dressed in his best armor." Crimson entered the room, shutting the door behind her. Her offer of help steadied me and stopped the breakdown that was coming. As we worked together to get him dressed, she talked casually as if we weren't preparing my soul mate for his final journey, to the afterlife. "Do you think the rain will let up soon?"

I looked up at her, confused. "Why would it? The gods and warrior spirits are mourning his death just as we are. It makes sense that it's raining."

There was a crash of thunder and lightning lit up the room before plunging us into a darkness that the fire in the hearth couldn't completely touch. I found the dark comforting. It hid how gray Thor's skin was. I could almost imagine that he was just asleep when I couldn't see clearly. It made the preparations easier.

After he was completely dressed, I looked around the room. "Where's Mjolnir?"

Crimson's brows furrowed. "It should be here. No one is able to lift it except Thor. I will ask if anyone has seen Mjolnir."

She had a point. Mjolnir was Thor's weapon. No one was able to lift it. I didn't remember seeing it when we returned to Thunder Valley. When the realization of what happened to it hit me, I felt like my chest was being crushed from the tightness. My breath caught in my throat as the back of my eyes burned with the tears that were building there.

"No need. Mjolnir is still at New Olympus. Thor dropped it when he was attacked. I didn't think to bring it home." I fisted my hand to my stomach, trying to force the nausea to subside. "He needs Mjolnir. He can't move on without it. No one can bring it to him though."

Crimson wrapped her arm around my shoulders. "Fear not, child. His spirit will take care of it."

***

I stood on the balcony attached to the Great Hall, staring down at the pyre that was made for Thor. It was tall. It took several men to move him up to the top of it. Once he was laid there, the courtyard fell silent. There wasn't a voice in the wind and the rain pounded on the onlookers. All eyes were on Thor.

You could hear the hearts of the people breaking as they waited for the ceremony to start. The loss of their king, protector, and savior weighed heavily. It was a loss that spread wide and far. Looking up, I could see people outside the walls as well. Paying their respects.

Thunder rolled continuously. Lightning danced across the sky. Rain came down in sheets. I could feel it pounding on my skin. There were little pinpricks of pain where the rain hit my skin, but I barely noticed. It was nothing compared to the pain in my chest.

With a deep breath, I tried to gather the courage I needed for what was next. "I'm not going to stand here and tell you all what a great warrior Thor was. We all know. Everyone here feels his loss. We will honor him tonight as the great warrior he was. If Valhalla still stood, he would be welcomed into the great walls. I, for one, am grateful that I had the chance to fight at his side. Let us begin. Archers, ready your arrows. May your aim be true."

All around the walls, I could see the arrows alight with fire. As the first arrows left their bows and sailed toward the pyre, I wished that I wasn't standing there watching it. This wasn't supposed to be how my marriage ended. He was supposed to still be by my side.

My heart wrenched and stopped when the arrows hit their mark. Fire started to lick up the timber that made the pyre. My throat clogged with the scream to stop stuck in it. I couldn't let myself stop it. Stopping the process would dishonor his memory. This is what he would have wanted.

As the second set of arrows shot out and hit the pyre, thunder crashed directly above our heads and lightning struck a tree, causing it to split in half with sparks shooting from it. Gasps and screams came from the crowds of people closest to the tree, as another bolt of lightning struck the ground next to the pyre.

Bolt after bolt struck around the pyre as thunder rumbled and growled, creating a vibration on the balcony. The flames licked up the wood of the pyre as the thunder and lightning increased. The rain came down impossibly harder. There was a loud crack in the air as something came flying out of the sky. Suddenly, the pyre exploded.

A scream of grief and fear ripped out of me as I watched pieces of the pyre scatter on the ground. That wasn't supposed to happen. Then a thought struck me. What happened to Thor? There should be body parts everywhere like the pyre. The body hadn't yet been touched by the flames when it exploded.

I looked around frantically, trying to figure out what was going on. Nothing was making sense. I could barely see where the pyre had been standing from the rain coming down so hard. A hand rested on my shoulder, causing me to whirl around, fist balled. I had every intention on knocking whoever dared to touch me on their ass.

I froze in shock with my fist pulled back, as I stared at the man behind me. There he stood, as majestic as he had been the day I first met him. The only difference was his hair was flat from the rain. I blinked several times, thinking that he was going to disappear once I did.

"You . . . you. . . You're dead." I stammered as I looked into the eyes of the man I loved. "I held you while you died."

He put a finger to my lips and smiled. "Do I look dead?"

I studied him. He didn't look dead, but I had seen him. I dressed him for the ceremony. I held him as he took his last breath. "How?"

"Kara. I do not know. I couldn't have been dead, but if you insist I was, then someone or something brought me back."

I was still unnerved and hesitant to touch him. With a shaky hand, I reached out and brushed the hair out of his eyes. I slid my hand from the side of his face, down his neck to his chest. I placed my hand flat on his chest to feel his heart beating underneath it. His heart beat steady and strong under my hand.

I smiled and threw my arms around his neck, pulling him down so I could press my lips to his. They were warm and alive. When he pulled his head from mine, I just stared at him.

"I believe, my darling wife, that whatever happened was because of you. Look, the rain has stopped." Thor looked up to the sky and my gaze followed his. He was right. The rain, which had been coming down since he died, had stopped and the sun finally showed its face.

The sound of cheering caused me to turn and face the crowd that was watching us. I pulled him forward and held our joined hands in the air.

"He lives!" I screamed for everyone to hear. The cheers roared to a deafening level. There were chants of long live the king echoing through the courtyard.

His arm came around me as he raised Mjolnir in the air. That must have been what came out of the sky before the pyre exploded, but I didn't care. I had Thor back and I wasn't going to take it for granted.

CHAPTER 29

I stood at the window of my bed chamber wrapped in a sheet. I was staring out at the rising sun. Hands caressed my shoulders, then lips touched my neck.

"Come back to bed, wife," Thor purred in my ear.

I leaned back into him, letting him share his strength with me. "Sorry to wake you, I needed to think."

"What woke me was that my wife was no longer by my side where she belongs. What ails you this morn?"

"Them," I nodded out to the courtyard where the Valkyries were starting their morning training.

"What of them?" he asked, his arms sliding around my waist.

"They need a home. I know I no longer belong in the ranks, but they are lost. They need Valhalla."

"You are a queen, a goddess now, Kara. Give them what they need."

"I'm no goddess." I instantly rejected that idea. "I'm simply a Valkyrie who found love."

His grip tightened on my waist. "No, you aren't simply a Valkyrie. You are more. I don't remember what happened after the snake attacked me, but if you say I was dead, then I was. It also means that you brought me back. You brought the rain with your mood. You are much more than a Valkyrie, or a wife.

You have always had that power inside you. You just had to find it."

His complete belief in me and my abilities made me want to believe. I gave a nod. "Then I will."

"You will later today. Right now, your husband is hungry for his wife."

He picked me up and carried me back to our bed. When he toppled onto it, careful not to land on me, I only had moments to start to formulate a plan for the new Valhalla before my mind went back to my husband and the way he was nibbling on my body.

***

We stood at the edge of the sea, my hands held out palms up. I had been practicing how I would do this for months before I was ready to try to use magicks that I wasn't sure I had. I closed my eyes and concentrated on what I wanted. A safe place for my Valkyries. A place for them to take the warrior souls that were collected after battles. A new Valhalla.

There was a pulling of power coming from me as I tried to create the island I was imagining. A hand landed on my shoulder. Thor. He was loaning me some of his strength. Behind me, I could hear Crimson chanting softly, also aiding me in power.

The sound of waves splashing against the surf increased and I could feel the spray from it. When I opened my eyes, they widened in wonder as the island appeared from under the surface of the water. When it fully came into view, I dropped my hands and panted, trying to catch my breath.

"Now, it is time to rebuild." I turned to Sanngrid. "We will rebuild for Brynhild."

She nodded. "Yes. We will have what we had before. All because of you, Kara."

"No. Not because of me. We will have it because of those who died in the battle. The ones who sacrificed their lives to ensure that we would be free and able to do so. We will rebuild and fight, because that is what we do. We are fighters. We will honor those we lost. We will bring their souls' home. To Valhalla."

Silence fell as light from the sun shone on the island and a building began to rise and form on its surface. We watched in reverence as Valhalla began to rise again.

About the Author

Elizabeth Reynolds, a born and bred native of Missouri, resides in a small town with her two boys and cats. When she isn't writing, she likes to spend time with her children and do some reading.

Elizabeth has also written under the name Zizi Cole. She is a writer of horror, and more recently, has branched out into the realm of fantasy. She's been an active member in the Indie community- making the best-seller list in her categories, she has also been nominated for several awards including "Best Horror Author". Her DAMNED series also took third place for "Best Horror" with Wild Dreams Publishing.

WORKS BY ZIZI COLE

The DAMNED Series

Sweet Nightmares

Sweet Visions

Sweet Conflict

Stand Alone Works

Heartless

Now I Lay Me down to Sleep

Black Zodiac

The Missing

Connected

Other works

The Princes' Collection

Afflicted

Unspoken

Wished